The Hanukkah Hook-Up

A Matzo Ballers Hanukkah Romance
Book 1

Jessica Topper

lunabloom

This is a work of fiction. Names, characters, places, and incidents either are the product of the author's imagination or are used fictitiously, and any resemblance to actual persons, living or dead, business establishments, events, or locales is entirely coincidental.

Edited by JoAnn Collins, Twin Tweaks Editing
Cover design by Amanda Usen

ISBN: 978-1-953863-11-9 (print)
978-1-953863-10-2 (e-book)

For Amanda Usen –
who brings light and joy to my soul all year long!
My partner in crime and carrot muffins,
and a true Matzo Baller for life

And in memory of Paul Green –
who always loved a good pun.

Preface

Amanda Usen and I began brainstorming the Matzo Baller series in 2021 and writing the books in earnest in September of 2023.

Then the world changed.

These books are a celebration of Judaism, and our mission is to bring more light and love into the world—now more than ever.

Chapter One

"Ho, ho, ho-ly crap...is that Nora Ruben, actually gracing us with her presence this year?"

Santa slapped white-gloved hands to his rosy cheeks in mock surprise, knocking his fake mustache/beard combo askew in the process.

Despite her less-than-cheery mood, Nora had to laugh. "Yes, a true holiday miracle." She glanced around Britesmith Hospitality Group's reception area, marveling at its transformation from everyday corporate gray to winter wonderland. "Where's the nearest bar?"

During her five-years-and-counting at Britesmith's headquarters, Nora always managed to beg off from the planning, attending, and clean-up of the annual event, due to the infamous Matzo Baller cruise usually coinciding the same night. She never experienced FOMO about the company holiday party; not when she had the eight-hour floating extravaganza hosted by her best friend's brother to look forward to, popping corks with the Who's Who of New York Jews lucky enough to score an ticket.

This year, Jay's party boat and Talia would be sailing

tonight without her, all because of some hayseed from the Iowa corporate office stirring up drama.

Talk about major FOMO.

"If you need a quick fix, Mrs. Claus from Marketing is mixing up some mean Yule Mules over near the windows. And the elves from IT are by the elevators, serving Peppermintinis. I myself prefer the Barracuda Lounge, thatta way." Santa thrust a thumb over his shoulder toward downtown.

"Thanks, Parker." Her assistant had totally blown his cover with the suggestion of the venerable Chelsea gay bar. He must've drawn the short straw around the water cooler this year to don the rented red suit.

"That's Mister Claus to you, young lady." He blew her a kiss. "And if that dress comes in multiple colors, I command you to buy at least two."

She swept her hands along the waistline of the Shoshanna jet-black crepe gown. The elegant strapless contraption was her consolation prize, courtesy of Rent the Runway. She had been coveting the dress for months, with its contrasting satin bodice in the perfect shade of blue. *Hanukkah blue*, she'd decided. If Tiffany could have its own hue, then the two-thousand-plus-year-old holiday had the right to claim a shade, too.

An oversized, yet understated bow detail along the side created a gathered look, making her feel like the perfect present. Nora sighed. It would've looked great on the deck of the Matzo Baller, against the glittery Manhattan skyline.

"Putting it on my wish list. Maybe Hanukkah Harry will come through."

Buy at least two, my ass. Britesmith didn't pay her nearly enough to buy one. She'd had to dip into her Florida February vacation fund for the rental gown.

Even if she could justify the price tag by wearing it

more than once over the eight nights of Hanukkah, something else would have to be sacrificed. Like half a month's rent...which really wouldn't fly, now that Libby was moving out.

At least her end-of-the-year bonus would cover that shortfall until she could find a replacement. And make working all weekend to prep for Team Hayseed's arrival a little more bearable.

Time for that mule.

Alex Beckman stood near the entryway, trying to blend in. Not an easy feat, seeing as every other co-worker either wore an ugly Christmas sweater, or was trying to out-sexy the sexy Mrs. Claus from the next cubicle over. He was a bit surprised, considering how much of a melting pot New York City was. He'd expected the Manhattan office's holiday party to not be so–

"*So this is Christmas...*"

A group of women swayed and sang, nearly sloshing their crushed candy-cane-rimmed martini glasses all over his suit. Tinsel seemed to be their accessory of choice, although one had mini Christmas light bulb earrings that flashed in time to the classic song they were currently butchering.

He'd expected Manhattan to color with more than just the red and green crayons from the Crayola box.

Alex took another sip from his copper cup. At least the drinks were ice cold, and the vodka premium. It was currently warming the pit of his stomach, empty save for the package of pretzels he'd consumed on the plane. The sugared cranberries were a nice touch, but he had tossed the useless green sprig of whatever the garnish was before it poked him up the nose.

Jewish guy problems...

He probably should've just waited until Monday to visit the office. Get – and give – a better first impression. But the CEO's idea of welcoming him to town had included hijacking the company car sent to the airport and detouring him here.

To this holly jolly nightmare.

Cocktail tables draped in red and green cloth enlivened the corporate landscape. Each had a plastic tea candle and poinsettia centerpiece. Some poor lacky played Santa in the corner, a faux snow path leading to his gilded chair. The karaoke girls were now taking turns perching on his lap, roaring with laughter and taking selfies.

Christmas was still almost a week away, and tonight was the first night of Hanukkah. Alex had hoped the last-minute assignment would've gotten his mind off the fact that it was the first holiday without his grandfather. But even without any trace of the Festival of Lights, the thought kept bobbing to the surface, like the cranberries in his drink.

A group of guys were doing shots by the DJ booth on the company's dime. Their loosened ties and rolled shirt-sleeves told Alex they'd wasted no time punching out early on a Friday afternoon to get the party started. They seemed like the happy-go-lucky sort that might even call him over to bond and throw one back.

Come Monday, their personnel files – and their fates – might very likely be in his hands.

Forget blending in with the red and green. He may as well have been dressed as the Angel of Death tonight.

"Beck!" Ron Hedstrom clapped him on the shoulder, using Alex's nickname like they were boyhood pals. One

Chicago conference after the acquisition last year did not make them pals. "Dig in, and don't worry. Those appetizers won't be flowing all night. We have a budget line for all of this."

"Not worried in the least. It all looks amazing." At least the food didn't appear to be Christmas-themed. Alex grabbed a stuffed mushroom from a passing tray. "And you seem to have a real great team. Thanks for having me." He surveyed the room, willing himself not to mentally count heads that might end up on the chopping block.

"Thrilled to hear you took an earlier flight. Nothing like a weekend in the city during the holiday season. In fact..."

Alex's gaze came to rest near the makeshift mule bar. David Bowie's "Little Drummer Boy" and whatever Hedstrom was saying fell to a whisper. His vision tunneled, only taking in the stunner in blue and black.

All the Christmas camouflage in the world couldn't hide her.

She craned her neck to examine the tray of hors d'oeuvres presented to her, smiling as she deftly plucked her selection and a cocktail napkin. All the while chatting with a Mrs. Claus who had decided to go for the goth look.

He liked the way her dark hair fell in soft waves to one side, leaving a pale collarbone exposed. And he could finally appreciate the abundance of white twinkling lights, as they highlighted her curves trussed up in that shiny blue ribbon.

Alex had the crazy urge to brush by and tug that dress bow, to see if he could unravel her. His fingers twitched. Just the thought replaced the warmth of the vodka, and aimed for a few degrees lower than his belt.

"Orange glazed meatloaf lollipop?"

Nothing like a pretentious finger food to draw you back

to reality. "I'm sorry, Ron. You were saying?" Alex selected one from the tray being proffered by the catering staff for good measure, giving him something to do with his free hand.

"I asked if you had family in town. Someone to show you the sights?"

"Actually, yes – I flew in early to catch a Hanukkah harbor cruise with my cousin, but..." *But as usual, Drew flaked out over a girl, and there went the extra ticket.* "...he had a change of plans. Not a big deal. I'll manage."

Alex had looked into procuring a ticket of his own, but it was quite the hot event, apparently sold out months ahead of time.

"I'm sure you'll make the most of your time here. Oh, and speaking of 'time' and 'managing,' there's someone I'd like you to meet."

"Who's the suck-up talking to Hedstrom?" April asked. "No one willingly hangs out with the CEO."

"No clue." Nora finished the last bite of quinoa and spinach puff, and dabbed her lips. "Although I saw some guys from the Westchester office earlier, so..."

"So you came to hide behind the shortest person in the room?" The graphic designer smirked. Even in her cherry red stacked Doc Martens, April barely hit the five-foot-two mark. But she still managed to look every guy in the eye.

"Not hiding." Nora scanned the room. "Just not interested in mingling with the Bridge and Tunnel crowd."

The guys from upstate thought the girls in the city office were easy. And used their train schedules as a lame excuse to "just crash at your place." It didn't matter if they were C-

Suite or Mailroom. It was a predictable song-and-dance that perhaps was the highlight of some other working girls' weekends, but not Nora's.

"Sorry you are missing the first night of Hanukkah for this," April scrunched her septum-pierced nose in consolation. "At least your holiday lasts eight days."

True. But the Matzo Baller was always the highlight. The thing she used her precious Floating Holiday time for, and not just because it was delightfully appropriate.

Nora drained the dregs of her mule. Fran from Marketing may have looked the part of sweet North Pole Nana with her gray wig and fake square glasses, but she had a heavy pour when it came to the vodka. Even still, Nora's second one had gone down way too easy. A rosemary stalk was a dangerous garnish, however. She chucked it toward a nearby trashcan, taking a stealth glance toward the stranger across the room as she made the shot.

"I think that guy just saluted me with his...meat pop."

April snorted, taking a little bite of the candy rim on her martini glass. "On that note...I'm going to track down more kosher fare for you."

"It's not a big deal!" Nora protested. In fact, she rarely thought about it. Yes, she had grown up in a Kosher household. And being a broke college student had pretty much turned her into a vegetarian by default. But she had made her peace with breaking the dietary law years ago; there was too much good ethnic food in the city to pass up.

And bacon. Bacon was her "gateway meat" – the *treif* that first led her astray, all thanks to Christophe. Her first boyfriend in a long string of boyfriends her mother would give a silent *oy vey* over whenever Nora brought them home. According to the Book of Ruth Ruben: *It's just as easy to fall in love with a Jewish man...*

"Ruben! Meet Beckman." Hedstrom was bearing down on her, drink sloshing precariously. Somewhere between Peppermintinis two and five, her boss had donned an elf hat. It slouched off the side of his shiny bald head, making him look more like a court jester than Santa's helper. "Beckman, Ruben. Now all you need is a Cohen and you'd have yourselves a law firm," he guffawed.

Nora sidestepped, and threw out a preemptive hand. All *she* needed was to add a hefty Manhattan dry cleaners' bill on top of this non-Baller weekend. Insult to–

Her spike heel caught and rolled on something beneath her. The room tilted, and her ears rang as she pinwheeled her arms frantically to catch her balance.

A solid grip anchored her elbow, and she felt the sear of five fingertips through satin spanning her waist. Instinct had her clutching the biceps of the only guy in the room wearing a full suit, other than her boss. And Santa.

"*Ope!* Close call." His murmur had humor and a hint of vodka lacing it. "You okay?"

So much for not mingling with the B&T crowd. She was practically tangoing with this one. Her traitorous heels still only brought her view to the guy's chin, carefully cultivated stubble and all. He was either hiding a dimple or a smirk under there, and Nora couldn't decide if that irked or intrigued her.

"No need to call OSHA. I'm fine."

He was still literally palming her ribcage. Adrenaline sent heat through her limbs and up to her hairline, and she considered hiding behind the tabletop poinsettias for the rest of the evening. Perfect camouflage.

"Ruben's a tough cookie," Hedstrom slurred. "Leave it to our HR trailblazer!" He turned to the small group that had gathered. "I've never had to sign an accident report form during a company Christmas – er-um, *holiday* party."

Nora cringed inwardly. The politically-correct afterthought was worse than the original oversight, in her opinion. And unnecessary. She'd lived her twenty-six years keenly aware that her holiday was minor in comparison to the big C.

Her tango partner looked like he shared her sentiment. His thick brow knit in a quizzical, apologetic way, and his warm dark eyes channeled...something. Sympathy? He dropped his hands when their eyes met, and Nora felt the absence. She hadn't pegged him as shy, but his gaze was now aimed at the carpet.

With a shaky breath, she smiled at her co-workers and regained her composure. Now that the commotion had subsided, they were back to getting their drink on. Whatever Hedstrom's earlier mission had been, he had aborted it in favor of the shrimp cocktail tower and talking to the IT guys with his mouth full.

"Ah, your nemesis." Her rescuer had deftly dropped to a knee and scooped something up, but now rose again to his full height. He rolled the shiny object between his finger and thumb before offering it to her.

Not shy, she noted. *Observant.*

"That would've made for an interesting work comp case – disabled by jingle bell."

So it hadn't been her ears ringing, after all. All this holiday stuff was hazardous to her health.

"Thanks for the quick save. I'm Nora."

"Beck. My pleasure."

A clanging ensued from the far side of the room. "You guys know what to do!"

Fran from Marketing had left her mule station, despite

the line, and was banging two empty copper cups together to get everyone's attention for some reason.

"Come on, don't be shy!" She sing-songed, as those around murmured in agreement.

"Any idea what's going on?"

Beck gave a baffled grin, shaking his head. "Not a clue."

Moses Almighty, he was cute. There was definitely a dimple under his scruff. Looking up at that smile was like basking in the sun. She could just close her eyes and–

Wait. Was that mistletoe above his head?

Nora had never paid attention to the stuff before. Not her circus, not her monkeys.

But now?

Now, a huge bunch was tied with a red ribbon to the Edison bulbs merrily strung haphazardly across the room. And the two of them just happened to be standing right under it.

"Jewish, remember?" Nora called to her co-workers. "Impervious to your Kryptonite."

Booing ensued.

"That's got to be a fire hazard," Beck murmured, glancing up at the sprigs of green.

Fran stared disapprovingly over her Mrs. Claus glasses at them.

"Okay, this is awkward."

Good, Nora. Lean into him – oops no, lean into it. *Acknowledge that elephant in the room.*

"Kind of like the time the Kiss Cam landed on me at a ball game..." He paused for effect. "...next to my sister's wife."

Okay, maybe the elephant in the room was the fact that she hadn't kissed or been kissed since Q3 of last year. And this guy was making her laugh – which *was* her Kryptonite. Her weakness – and a huge turn-on.

"And what exactly does kissing on demand have to do with Christmas?" she added under her breath, more for Beck's benefit.

"I don't think we can question their customs...considering we dip our pinkies in wine to ward off plagues and open doors for invisible prophets," he murmured, close to her ear. "Not to mention throw perfectly good bread into the river for *Tashlich*."

She loved that he had just referenced one of her favorite, more obscure parts of Rosh Hashanah, and had to admit...it felt good to be able to joke with someone at work who understood.

Yet *work* was the last place she wanted to let her guard down.

And this guy, dimple or not, was on the payroll with her.

Chapter Two

Itchy palms meant you were coming into money...at least that's what Alex's grandmother always said. That plus, *Itchy nose, Alexi...kiss a fool.* All Alex knew was his hands had just been somewhere precious and now they weren't. That bombshell dress could've been a potato sack of burlap compared to the silky underside of her arm where he'd caught her. Cool to the touch, yet his palms burned.

And had he been a total fool not to just embrace the holiday spirit and kiss her when he'd had the chance?

No, he was here on official work business – not to canoodle in the name of the infant baby Jesus. And Nora seemed to want to stay all business as well. Despite her conspiratorial good nature under that sprig of mistletoe... she'd stepped away just as quick.

*Nora...Nora Ruben...*Her name sounded familiar. He tried to place it from any of the company emails, spreadsheets and mountains of Britesmith paperwork he'd been buried in over the past week. When his uncle had tasked him with this mission, the New York 54 had been just that...

a number. A number he had to reduce by half, by year's end.

His grandfather had had big plans for the acquisition in New York; in fact, it had been the only thing lighting up his eyes for the past two years since losing his bride of sixty-eight happy ones. Myers and Sons, the family-owned food service and hospitality company, had chugged steadily along as a Midwest stalwart, making earnest livings for eight decades and three generations of Myers. "Not bad for a kid from the old neighborhood, selling his dad's peanuts at the ballgames," was his favorite way to end every story told to his grandson. Along with: "And someday, this can all be yours."

Can and not *will* – at least Grandpa My had left the door open for choice. His grandpa had been the last of "Sons" in the original Myers and Sons, and the one mainly responsible for diversifying the company's interests, from ballpark concessions to movie theaters to hotels. And now, with his New York vision realized, they had officially added Broadway and other entertainment landmarks throughout the city to their roster.

Too bad he hadn't lived long enough to see it.

"So. Beck..."

Her melodious voice brought him back to the here and now. He didn't mind Nora using his nickname one bit.

"First Manhattan office *holiday* party?"

Melodious...yet wry, hinting, and humorous. Her tone channeled what he could only imagine were years of calculated nonchalance about being called out as "the other."

He was no stranger to that. Not at work, mind you. Myers and Sons probably employed half the Jewish population of Des Moines. But growing up in the Midwest, much less Iowa? He'd been "othered" more times than he cared to count.

"What gave me away? I'll have you know I can ugly sweater with the best of them."

The way her dark eyes keenly appraised him revved a motor he swore had left him in the dust at the side of some gravel road years ago. But it was her laugh that truly did him in. Starting as an uninhibited burst and dwindling down to a throaty chuckle; it was dead sexy like the rest of her.

Who was this creature? He certainly had not expected her among the New York 54. He wanted to keep making her do that, indefinitely.

"You didn't get the memo about the mandatory red and green? It usually goes out the day after Thanksgiving."

"My assistant must've been slacking that day. Yours?"

"Mine is...oh my God."

Alex followed her gaze toward Santa, who had shed his red fur coat and the lap ladies in favor of dirty dancing in his tight A-shirt with a burly, bearded elf who was at least a head taller.

"Lumberjack Herbie or Six-Pack Santa?"

"Parker really does like to show those off any chance he gets. But that's his ex, Nolan from IT." She groaned. "Definitely naughty list material."

"'Tis the season for...giving, I guess." Alex tactfully suggested, as mock-spanking ensued.

"It's like a Bing Crosby/Magic Mike mashup I can't quite look away from."

"It's beginning to look a *latke* like Christmas!" The goth she-Claus was back, bearing a tray of mini-potato pancakes, each with a dollop of sour cream on top. No applesauce, but they were studded with salmon roe and capers, according to a tiny placard. In keeping with the red and green theme, Alex supposed.

"Is caviar kosher?" The girl looked to both of them for guidance.

"Depends on who you ask...and on the type of fish. Okay by me," Alex said.

"April, stop! Gimme." Nora took one. She popped the bite-size carb between her lips. "Not exactly the work of the Jewish Grandmother, but close enough."

Her job seemingly done, April awarded custody of her tray to Alex before tripping off in her tiny combat boots toward the makeshift dance floor.

"Any port in a storm," he murmured, picking one from the tray as well. "*L'chaim.*" He toasted in her direction.

Slightly crispy, the cool dairy tempering the hot oil. The unexpected briny pop of the roe and capers was...different, but not horrible. Not that his own gran would approve, mind you.

"Speaking of ports...has Port Chester heard any rumors about Q1?"

Luckily he was still chewing; he needed a beat. Was Port Chester the upstate office? And how much had Hedstrom let on to her about the purpose of his visit? Even as CEO, the guy didn't know the half of it.

His Uncle Marty had taken up the mantle the minute Grandpa My's *shivah* period was over and began making drastic changes to the company, slashing budgets as resolutely as he had cut into the black mourner's ribbon on his left suit lapel. He had also given Alex the list currently burning a hole in his pocket of the New York employees to be "made redundant" by Myers and Sons' buyout of Britesmith.

"Or are you one of the lucky few still in the Jersey

branch?" Nora continued, leaning to pluck another latke from the tray he held close to his chest. Her perfume was subtle but brought him back to the here and now.

Oh wait, she was thinking he was a fellow soldier on the local front. Had his Midwestern accent not given him away? His automatic *ope*, an Iowa catch-all for politeness when he caught her from falling? He set the tray down. "I'm not –"

You're not cut out for this, Alex.

You're a Beckman, not a Myers.

"Attention...attention, just a minute of your time... everyone!" Hedstrom was gesturing, jumbo shrimp in his hand like a baton. His elf hat, Alex observed, was missing its jingle bell. "I could've shared this in an email, but figured since I had everyone here. You're all getting Christmas Eve off this year!" His proclamation was met with cheers. "That's the good news, folks. Unfortunately, the bonuses you've all been anticipating, well..."

Nora gripped the bell still in her palm, hard enough to make a mark. *He's got to be kidding.*

"But everyone gets a beautiful poinsettia to take home!"

All the ass-busting she had done all year. Just this quarter alone she had put in an average of sixty hours a week, and the fact that she had given up her weekend – *this* weekend, the weekend of the Matzo Baller – sacrificing in order to make her boss look good come Monday in front of Team Hayseed...

Christmas Eve off had been *her* idea. She and Parker had toiled over a whiteboard full of sticky notes, playing Jenga with every matinee and early curtain so that her staff could have some time with their families. Leave it to Hedstrom to take credit, yet he'd be just as quick to throw her under the bus when one of his schemes backfired.

Not that she cared about getting a pat on the back for it; at the end of the day, the only thing that mattered was work-life balance for her employees. As for herself?

She thought of her stifling little cube upstairs, far from any natural lighting. Her desk piled with folders that never seemed to move from incoming to outgoing. Her sad little plastic menorah perched, waiting for her to twist each "flame" on, marking the first three Hanukkah days as she toiled through them.

No one should have to spend half their waking hours in a three-sided fabric box every day. Let alone on a holiday weekend.

Nora grabbed her clutch off the table and wove through clusters of her co-workers. Their holiday spirit may have deflated somewhat, but for now they seemed content to nosh on company time. The strong drinks probably helped, too.

Not a minute more for her, though.

As she pushed past Hedstrom, she resisted the urge to plunk his discarded jingle bell into the half-full Peppermintini in his hand.

Better to let him choke on his own regret come Monday morning when the mess he should've handled months ago came crashing down. No longer her problem.

Nope, not one second more.

There was a boat she needed to catch.

Nora Ruben.

Of course her name would be at the top of his goddamn list.

Alex had stepped into the hall to get some air, after Hedstrom sucked the room of it with that horrible news. And why had the guy looked directly at the stunner in blue and black when he announced it?

Alex didn't bother looking at the rest of the names before stashing the paper back into his pants pocket. Was it coincidence the CEO had led him right to Employee One and introduced them?

Sheila, his ex-girlfriend who had been raised on a farm, once told him you never named the animals intended for slaughter. *Name them and you form a connection with them.*

Easy for her to say – not so easy when your ancestors were tattooed with numbers and herded into cattle cars.

Wow, Alex. Life of the party here.

Even without a business degree, Alex knew certain jobs and departments overlapped and became redundant during M&As. And as his uncle had reminded him before he boarded the plane: "This kind of thing happens all the time in the private-sector, Alex. Employment 'at-will' is Business 101 stuff."

They had disagreed on how to handle the layoffs from the start. Marty was focused on the numbers – specifically, how the gross salaries of the twenty-seven New York employees who'd landed on the list conveniently matched with his projections for next year's budget, once erased.

Alex wanted to see the inner workings of the office come Monday, and make determinations without the bias of such a list.

Then again, he had once taken apart an entire piano because he wanted to see how it worked. It had been a bigger job than anticipated.

And bloodier. Piano wires were sharp.

You're in and out in one day, kid. Numbers. Hand over the list and no one gets hurt.

He didn't need his Uncle Marty in his head right now. He needed to get back to the holiday party, make those connections. Because even he could tell something didn't add up when it came to Britesmith.

And he definitely didn't want to think about the list. Not when Nora Ruben was making a beeline out of the party and right toward him.

Chapter Three

"Hey, you want to get out of here?"

He was kind of cute, for a Bridge and Tunnel guy. Even as he had tried not to choke on that latke-lookalike earlier. Hers was sitting like lead in the pit of her stomach, after Hedstrom's little speech.

No bonus.

No half the rent from Libby.

No Florida February.

Leave it to our trailblazer.

"Lead the way, Ruben."

She liked the way Beck called her that. Not like Hedstrom, who used her surname as a punchline. Coming from Beck, it felt as if they had been in the trenches for years together; not like two quasi-strangers who just happened to be on the same payroll. Whose paths would only cross at the random corporate retreat or quarterly team-builder.

Or holiday parties from hell.

She also liked the feel of his suit sleeve brushing against her bare arm as they made their way into the mezzanine.

"Let me grab my coat upstairs and – oh, hell. Never mind."

The elevator banks teemed with people. It looked like every other business tenant in the building had sent representatives down to scope out Britesmith's party. And help themselves to the drinks.

Then again, it was corporate rush hour, on a Friday night.

"Shall we walk up?" Beck had found the stairwell door and pushed it open.

Bless his heart, in these heels?

"My office is ten floors up." Nora laughed, her hand stopping his on the handle. Britesmith had its mezzanine-level reception area and conference room, meant to impress. But a sad honeycomb of cubicles in the sky was the fate of its worker bees. "No skyscrapers in your suburbia, I assume?" she teased.

"Of course there are. The sky's just...a little higher here."

Correction: he was *really* kind of cute for a Bridge and Tunnel guy. She liked how he gave her a roll of those dark eyes, and how they lit up at her teasing.

"Don't look now, but..."

Too late. She looked.

More mistletoe dangled from the EXIT sign above the door to the stairwell. April had tried to cajole her into helping decorate earlier in the day, claiming short girl problems. Apparently she had enlisted someone, because the green stuff was everywhere.

When in Rome...or perhaps the North Pole?

Beck's lips perfectly parted in surprise when her mouth touched down, featherlight. But they soon recovered and claimed her, as did his fingers, threading through her hair and pulling her closer.

"Now I get what all the fuss is about," he breathed, capturing her top lip between both of his. "This stuff should hang all year round."

"Shhh, let's just keep culturally appropriating, please."

His laugh rumbled deep, and she felt it against her chest as she leaned in. "They did take our latkes, after all."

"And there're way more people at the movies and out for Chinese these days on Christmas," Nora pointed out. "We used to have that all to ourselves."

Beck was gazing down at her, like he wanted to have *her* all for himself. "You're right, way more crowds. Speaking of which..."

Ah, right. Their quick getaway had turned deliciously slow, pinned against the fire-door. And now the lobby swelled with even more revelers.

A weighted warmth spread across her bare shoulders. "Take mine. Let's get out of here." Nora gratefully slipped her arms into the oversized suit jacket. Its silky lining held his body heat and a sweet-spiced scent that she could get quickly addicted to if she wasn't careful.

Had they both temporarily lost their minds? Making out with a co-working stranger in some dark corner at the office holiday party had *not* been on Nora's wish list for Hanukkah Harry. And Beck, well, he didn't seem to be the usual B&T guy looking to score with a city girl.

They didn't even have the excuse of some dark corner – no, they had just gone full-on teenage make-out session in the illuminated exit stairwell, in all its fluorescent-lit glory.

For a girl who barely shared her weekend plans with any colleagues besides April and Parker, she had certainly put on a good show-and-tell tonight.

It was definitely time to get out of there.

"Follow me."

There was a rhythm to Manhattan crowds, indoors and out. As people tunneled closer, arms pinned at their sides and everyone inching toward the same goal, Nora turned her palm up and reached back. The press of Beck's fingertips on hers was immediate, as if he had been instinctively reaching forward.

They had skyscrapers in downtown Des Moines, all right... the Ruan Center, 801 Grand, and the HUB Tower all housed scores of people; but nothing like this.

Alex's head was spinning, but not just from the Manhattan crowds and bracing wind. That kiss Nora had laid on him was mind-erasing. His name, his legacy, what he was even doing here in the first place...

He certainly hadn't come to New York to hook up with anyone from the office, *in* the office building that would soon have his family's name on it. He shouldn't have let that happen. It just complicated things further. Yet at that moment, he would've been perfectly happy to send them both back through the revolving door and inside to continue it.

But Nora seemed to have something else in mind.

"You don't get seasick, do you?" she asked, stepping to the curb and hailing a cab impressively quick. "Pier 83, please."

With that slit up her dress and those heels, no wonder she stopped traffic.

"Nah, all good." His cousin did, though – thinking of Drew made him think of the sold-out cruise. "You wouldn't happen to know anything about a Hanukkah boat ride happening?"

The streetlights lit the flecks in Nora's brown eyes as the taxi whisked them downtown. "Oh, it's way more than a boat ride. Eight hours, under twenty bridges, past a hundred landmarks, completely circling Manhattan? It's a total Baller. And I'm a VIP for life."

"You are full of surprises, Ruben."

"You ain't seen nothing, Beckman." Nora arched one perfectly-sculpted brow his way.

Smiling, she pulled her phone from her handbag. "I'm texting them to hold the boat."

Who was this girl? Other than the name on the top of his hit list?

Her boss had called her one tough cookie and a trail-blazer. But ever since Nora had blazed a trail right out of that office party, she seemed a different person. Hedstrom had clearly upset some part of her ecosystem with that speech, and Alex had the feeling it wasn't the free poinsettia that did it. No, it was what he was *taking*.

Who withdraws a promised year-end bonus, two weeks before the year-end?

He'd seen all of Britesmith's Profit & Loss statements and balance sheets; nothing he recalled to warrant such a blow to employee morale.

Alex took the opportunity to check his phone as well. He groaned inwardly, seeing two missed calls and a text from his uncle. *Off the clock, Marty.* Although were you ever really off the clock when it was your family business? Even on Hanukkah?

Just remember: we Myers deal with numbers all the time.

Use your head.

Not his Beckman heart, apparently.

Nora's phone jangled to life in her hand. "Hey, Jay. Yeah...uh-huh. I know...*I know.*" She gave an eyeroll. "Because I temporarily lost my mind, alright?" He liked that her hint of an accent got a tad bit stronger with the sass. "Long story. Nope. Just two. Awesome. *Mwah,* love you!"

Alex had read up on the bridges and landmarks and all the amenities of the chartered StarLine cruise ship. And about the communal candle lighting to kick off the party. The Moët champagne towers. The DJ, the live bands. And the food prepared by a different hot-shot chef each year. But nothing about anyone named Jay.

He thumbed a text over to Drew.

Hey scored pass to boat after all. See you soon. Do you know a Jay on board?

Dope! Girls on board SO money!

Drew's response was almost immediate. And useless. It didn't really answer the question. Who the hell was Jay?

It was stupid, Alex knew. To be jealous. He barely knew Nora. And what little he did know kept sparking warnings like a roadside flare anyway. *Trouble ahead – use caution.*

Yet, when he thought of all the ways he wanted to get to know her, the night seemed impossibly short.

Eight hours on a boat was a start.

Chapter Four

W*ho needed a runway when you had a gangplank?*

Nora gathered her dress so the hem wouldn't catch in her heels, feeling absolutely buoyant as they made their way up the metal footbridge. It practically folded up behind them, not a minute to spare.

She couldn't wait to see Talia. Jay, she knew, would give her shit and eventually ease up. But Talia would be over the moon at Nora's change of plans.

Change of brain-wiring, more like it.

"Weigh anchor!"

A horn blasted, and the passengers cheered. Warmly-lit windows welcomed them from every level; the celebration had clearly started a while ago. Music seemed to crystalize in the winter air.

Beck took her hand to help her over the last step, but didn't let it go right away. "Thank you...for making this happen, Nora."

It was the first time he'd called her that; she decided she

liked it even better. He drew out her name like it was something to be savored; something precious.

First kiss on land, second by sea...

Was it wrong that she was already thinking of all the places on board they could steal away to and snog?

"Actually, *I'm* the bad-ass mofo who made this happen..." A holler floated down from above. "But if taking credit helps Noraleh score, I'm all for it."

Jay Katz leaned over the upper deck rail, wearing a captain's hat and a smart-ass grin. The same grin that had calmed Nora's nerves at JFK when, at nineteen, she was about to board her first-ever international flight and leave everything and everyone she knew behind for a year in Israel.

"Avast! Stay right there, I'm coming down."

Leave it to Jay – the three-hundred-sixty-four other days of the year, he was just one of New York's notable live event promoters. But on Baller day, he let his pirate freak flag fly, lingo and all.

Nora turned to Beck. "I should've warned you. Half my Year-Course crew are probably on this boat. Did you do a gap year?"

"No, but I did Birthright a while back with my cousin Drew. Who's here tonight, too, by the way. That was only a ten-day trip. A year must've been incredible."

"It was something, all right." Nora laughed. What were the odds of walking the earth at the exact same time as the motley group she considered her found family; let alone all of them landing on the same kibbutz in the Negev desert?

Ugh, getting sappy was not Nora's MO for the night. The guys would make fun of her like days of old – Avi playing an overwrought version of *Dust in The Wind* on his battered acoustic guitar; Jonah pouring her another Arak over ice to shut her up. Jay farting in her general direction to lighten the mood. Eli philosophizing with some 'Grains of Sand' metaphor.

God, she didn't want to think about Eli Gold, tonight of all nights.

The girls would all get it, though. Talia especially. The term "ride or die" was particularly apt when the ride in question was a pack of spitting, suicidal camels.

An oversize hat came down firmly on her head, its brim falling over her eyes. "A minute later, kid. You're lucky it's the season of miracles."

"I owe you one, Jay." Nora righted the captain's hat in time to see Jay stick out a hand to Beck.

"Hey, man. Bar mitzvah theme?"

"Not this again." Nora groaned. "Beck, this is Jay Katz, the mastermind behind the Matzo Baller. And you don't have to answer that."

Beck, to his credit, didn't miss a beat. "Baseball."

Jay broke into an easy grin. "You can tell a lot about a person by their party theme. Take Noraleh here."

"No, Gatsby. We're not doing this."

Didn't this guy have a party to run? A boat to sail?

A short pier to take a long walk off?

"Sock monkey theme."

"It was not!" Nora insisted. "It was a Paul Frank theme. Who doesn't love Julius the Monkey?"

While she pleaded her case, Beck wasn't lobbing his glances between them like a spectator at a tennis match; no, he was studying her intently. She could only imagine what was going through his head at that moment.

Like a dog with a chew-toy, Jay refused to let it go. "You *say* Julius, because it's the more socially acceptable lifestyle choice. But we all know *Jocko* was your first love."

"Yes, sue me. I had a sock monkey growing up."

"Beck. She brought the thing to Israel. Jocko went everywhere we did. The Western Wall, to Egypt, *into* the Dead Sea...he stunk to high heaven after that."

"And whose fault was that?"

"It might've been Avi's? Anyway, RIP Jocko."

Nora snorted. "Says the guy who probably dug the shallow grave." Turning to Beck, she explained, "Jocko went MIA in the Middle East."

Jay laughed, holding up hands in innocence. "Gotta go check on what's taking that sister of mine so long with the eats."

He was already off, raking a hand through his mop of hair, pointing at some random guy who yelled his name in praise. Over one tuxedoed shoulder, he called back to them. "Candle lighting in five!"

Nora's friend Jay repeated those magic words into a mic moments later, and everyone on their deck level started hightailing it for the stairs. Ball gowns mixed with Boho, everyone chattering excitedly about the start of the holiday. More tuxedos and suits than jeans and ugly Hanukkah sweaters, but there were even a few of those.

Alex guided Nora into the ballroom, away from the stampede. Not exactly empty, but slightly more private.

"Ugh, sorry. Told you. That's Jay, in full effect. The annoying brother I never had."

She looked adorable, the big captain's hat pushed back on her head, making her eyes appear even more amplified. Were those...tears she was blinking back? But she was smiling a genuine smile as she pointed out her favorite elements of the room.

There was, indeed, a tower built of perfectly symmetrical champagne glasses. And slowly rotating above it, an aerialist suspended from the ceiling in silks; perfectly pouring from a Moët bottle a bubbly cascade to fill each and every one while onlookers gasped.

"On a moving boat. Crazy, right?" Nora laughed, shaking her head. "Jay pulls off magic, that fucker. And yes, Gatsby's black and white ball was indeed his theme as a bar mitzvah. I didn't know him back then, but I'm not surprised."

There was a jazz band in one corner, clusters of people swaying on the dance floor. Long buffet tables adorned with blue and gold awaiting their feast. And that was just one tier of the multi-leveled ship. Alex suspected every deck harbored a different feel and theme.

"And you almost missed all this, because of the work party?"

Nora crossed her arms, leaning against one of the pillars near the stocked bar. "Not the party, per se. Work, in general." She sighed. "Things that really shouldn't wait until Monday."

The sleeves of his suit jacket covered half her hands, sending a surge of possessiveness through him. Alex wanted to cover her; shield her from big brother-like teasing and boss bullies and any other unpleasantness that threatened to dim the spark in her eyes.

"I've had to do things for Hedstrom that I'm not proud of."

Alex felt a splash of dread and adrenaline mix a cocktail of panic in his gut.

"Let's just say you are lucky you aren't in his division,"

she continued. "Never take a transfer to my office, okay? I couldn't bear it."

In all the spontaneity of the night, it was easy to forget Nora had mistaken him for a co-worker. But it wasn't right for Alex to let her keep assuming that.

"Listen, about Britesmith..."

Two fingers touched down on his lips. Nora was on tiptoes. "Nooo. No work talk! I changed my mind. It's officially Shabbat, it's officially Hanukkah." She leaned in, her own lips resting against her fingers and their mouths just millimeters apart. "A pact," she murmured. "Neither of us talk about how miserable we are there, okay? And just enjoy..."

She slid her fingers down his chin, leaving no barrier between their lips, and Alex took full advantage. Nora may have instigated that first kiss, but he was taking responsibility for this one. And for making her knees buckle.

"The night?"

His lips followed the trail of her fingers, down the smooth hollow of her neck. His mouth on the tiny diamond *Chai* charm at her throat. He wanted to find all her sweet spots; the ones that made her intake of breath sharp, made her swear softly and pull him closer like she was doing now.

"Are you proposing...a Hanukkah hook-up, Ms. Ruben?"

That slit in her dress, her bare leg mincing between his thighs...the way she bit her lip and smiled. All signs pointed to yes. Not that those cues alone represented consent – Alex was fully aware of that.

"All I'm saying is...you and this party and that drink menu over there could contribute greatly to my not worrying about Monday morning. In that order."

Technically, he wasn't even supposed to be in town

until Monday. Couldn't he just set aside the tasks hanging over his head and let come what may, too?

"Well then, let's get the lady a..." He perused the cleverly-themed list of holiday drinks over her shoulder. "... Challah-day Hangover?"

She laughed, pushing him away and handing over Jay's hat. "Officially letting you steer the ship. You should at least say hi to your cousin. And I need to find Talia before the candles."

"Is that Jay's sister?"

"More like his secret weapon. And my bestie." She grinned. "Meet me at the menorah?"

There was that arch of her defined brow again, her smile turning into a secret shared just between them, before she headed for one of the many staircases.

What was the harm in a little Hanukkah fun and games? In a sparkling new city, with a dazzling girl?

And maybe one night of fire could last...the two-thousand-year old holiday had proven that.

Chapter Five

"Alexi! Bro! Dude!"

Drew bellied up to the bar, already lit like the eighth night. Alex hadn't seen his cousin since their grandfather's funeral, and was glad it was under happier circumstances tonight. But he really didn't want to have to babysit him through seasickness. Or alcohol poisoning. Or any combination of the two that might send them both heaving overboard.

The bartender slid Alex's drink order toward him, nodding in thanks for the tip slipped between the two glasses. He'd recommended the Eight-day Buzz to kick off the night.

"How's the head-chopping going, oh mighty Chosen One?"

Even under the happy-go-lucky guise of party boy, there was resentment in his cousin's tone. Why *was* he chosen over Marty Myers' own first-born son anyway? It was a mystery whose answer now lay six feet under.

"Fuck off. You know I wouldn't choose this, if given any choice."

That was the thing about family. And Jewish guilt.

You take care of Britesmith.

Honoring his grandfather's wish seemed to fly directly in the face of Uncle Marty's inheritance.

Protect New York, Alexi.

Like he was some damn superhero.

And following his uncle's orders of cleaning house – or as Drew called it, chopping some heads – made fiscal sense, but...something felt off.

Drew's dad and Alex's mom were siblings. Both growing up as Myerses, but with very different talents and values. His uncle, with a gift for numbers, respected in his conservative congregation, always there to lead a minyan. His mother, a free spirit artist who married a modest academic, and had raised their son to simply be a good person, not necessarily a good Jew.

Alex had loved and respected his grandfather so much, and the feeling had seemed mutual. Even while Alex avoided anything to do with the family business, holding it at bay for as long as he could, keeping it at arm's length while he explored his options and interests.

He'd thought that when the time came to decide, he'd have his grandfather there to consult with and mentor him.

Suddenly, the only mentor was Uncle Marty, who had probably envisioned his own version of Myers and Sons with Drew following in his footsteps. Drew Myers, a Wall Street guy who already had New York in his back pocket.

Not a Beckman. A dreamy, artsy Beckman.

"I'm just messing with you, cousin. So glad you're here. Have a Jelly Donut shot with me!"

"Can you make sure this gets back to its rightful owner?"

Alex passed the captain's hat over the bar to the bartender before turning to his cousin.

"Should you be mixing motion sickness meds with alcohol, Drewski?"

Silly how they resorted to the pet names their grandma had given them back in the day. Gran Leah was generous with her time and love, but she had no patience with the American names their parents had bestowed upon her ten grandchildren. She far preferred calling them some Eastern European variation; perhaps after a beloved childhood friend...or pet goat, for all they knew.

"Not on any meds, man! Get this." His cousin launched into one of his over-the-top, name-dropping stories, but all Alex could think about was getting back to Nora.

He'd never really cared all that much about the candle-lighting part of the holiday growing up – his dreidel game was strong and he had a sweet tooth motivating him to win all the chocolate gelt off his cousins before sundown. But he found himself wanting to hear his voice, in unison with Nora's, reciting the Hebrew blessing every Jew – even the most unobservant – could probably mumble in their sleep. He wanted to see how the flicker of the holiday lights lit up her eyes even brighter.

He'd never wanted to ditch his cousin so bad in all his life.

"So long story short, I ended up with both the pharmacist AND the acupuncturist!" Drew laughed. "Jess had to work tonight, being flu shot season and all. But I brought Dahlia along. She has no clue what's going on with this whole *mishegas*."

Two shots apparitioned atop the bar – this bartender was working all the miracles tonight, despite the crowd being three-deep. He was also rocking Captain Jay's hat.

"Well," Alex toasted. "To *mishegas*."

Forget about even getting near the menorah. The entire passenger manifest must've gotten the memo to gather around the giant hanukkiah – a twelve-foot candelabra Jay commissioned especially for the Matzo Baller. Taking no chances with an open flame on board, it was electric, but not like the big gaudy one lit in Brooklyn every year.

"Tal!" Nora's internal radar homed in on her best friend's head of ginger curls amongst the crowd. It was like having BFF-GPS and it worked every time. Talia was already near the tall ladder next to the menorah.

Jay had hired some kind of techno-klezmer band to kick off the quasi-religious portion of the festivities, and they broke into a trippy version of "Hava Nagila." She caught a glimpse of Beck on the outskirts of the crowd. He lifted the two drinks in his hand with a smile and a shrug. She toasted him back with her empty hand and mouthed *Sorry* – there was little chance he'd make it to her side of the boat without sloshing half those drinks on the deck, given the number of impromptu hora circles breaking out.

Some guy next to Beck helped himself to one of the drinks, much to Nora's surprise. *My cousin,* he mouthed. Rolling his eyes as the guy alternated yammering and drinking.

Nora wasn't going to get anywhere if she didn't hora her way there. She stepped into the fray, instantly regretting her shoe choice. Two women twice her age latched onto her, linking their arms through hers like that old Barrel of Monkeys game. Feet and hips minced side to side in a dance that felt ingrained since childhood. Just as her circle approached Beck's side of the deck, another faction serpentined through, going counter-clockwise at a dizzying rate.

Nora lost sight of him, keeping pace with the women in her group who were clearly trying to out-hora their frenemies, their mahjong league, and anyone standing in their way. Into the middle they all went, arms up, then back. Nora laughing till her sides hurt.

The group suddenly changed directions and widened. Talia had broken in, bless her. She stole Nora out and moved her to safety under the menorah before some overambitious guys began Cossack dancing and Kazotsky kicking their way into the center of the circle.

She longed to tell Talia about the strange turn of events the night had taken; complete with dumpster fire details about the office party and bringing a plus-one on board, but now was not the time or place. The lighting of the first candle officially kicked off the Festival of Lights and the Matzo Baller itself.

As emcee, Jay would do the honors of "lighting" the *shamash*, the helper candle that stood taller than the others, before lighting a candle representing the first night. After that, the menorah would reside in the ferry terminal and be lit by various city officials throughout the rest of the holiday until the entire thing shown like a beacon from Pier 83.

But first, it wouldn't be tradition if their crew didn't help hoist their Year-Course leader to the top of the ladder.

"Tradition...TRADITION!"

Avi Wolfson strut-shuffled across the deck like a tattooed Tevye, his booming baritone helping to part the crowd. Murmurs and cheers rose from those on board who realized the lead singer of the chart-dominating Painted Doors was in their midst, but no one tried to intercept him on his mission. In fact, the crowd parted as miraculously as the Red Sea.

It may have helped that Avi had a hulking henchman bringing up the rear – the friends all knew him as the softest teddy bear, but there was nothing "klein" about Jonah Klein; even as the youngest kid on their Israel trip, he towered over them. Although tonight, Jonah's intimidating stature and bodyguard vibes were softened a bit by the butt-ugly Hanukkah suit he wore. A print of neon dreidels, menorahs, and even jelly donuts and Chinese takeout containers danced across crushed black velvet.

"This is how we Jew it," he sang, bringing a little Def Jam style to go with Avi's *Fiddler on the Roof* kitsch. With a wink, he stabilized the last rung of the ladder with a solid grip so Jay was safe to climb the rest of the way up.

Nora had a flashback; the same four friends leaning against the rakes and shovels they held, each trying to make the others laugh harder under the glaring sun on the *moshav* farm they'd all worked on for the first three weeks of their year abroad. As Jay's voice echoed through the microphone, thanking everyone for coming, her brain fast-forwarded. These were the people she wanted holding the poles of her *chuppah* someday, if she ever got married. Lifting up and supporting her wedding canopy as they had her life, in the years since Israel.

Emotion filled her eyes and throat, and she tried to concentrate on the blessings Jay led. But Avi was doing that thing he did with his eyebrow every time Adonai was mentioned. And Jonah was grinning as he stumbled over the third, more obscure prayer. And Talia's voice lifted and carried them all, her Hebrew melodious and resolute.

Over her friend's shoulder, she finally caught sight of Beck again. His lips moving in unison with the words coming from hers. The smile he flashed her competed with the crowd's cheer as the stained glass flame on the first candle was officially illuminated. A group hug, starting with a J&J sandwich, ensued, and she lost sight of Beck again as Talia and Avi were pulled in.

"So, who's the suit?" Jay, his *shamash* duty done for the evening, was back to being up in everyone's business.

"A colleague with a sense of adventure who was just as eager to ditch a Christmas party as I was – and that's all *you* need to know," Nora supplied. Talia squeezed her hand, indicating girl talk later.

"I mean...who's the guy in the three-thousand-dollar suit and what's he want from you? I know Brioni when I see it, Nor."

Damn, take back the mailroom theory. Not that there was anything wrong with that.

"Kinda have to side with Katz on this one," Avi added. "You've got fifteen hundred dollars of this guy's wardrobe wrapped around you tonight, so...what's he expecting wrapped around him later?"

"Stop. He's been a perfect gentleman...he's fine. He's a co-worker. But we made a pact not to talk about work tonight."

"And since you are a workaholic, that is a losing bet for you. Lucky him," Jay quipped.

"God, you guys. Stop. Beck is..."

Who exactly *was* Beck? She realized she didn't even know his full name. It couldn't very well be Beck Beckman. Could it?

Great. She made out with some nicknamed co-worker. Twice tonight.

Might has well have been "guy in the third cubicle on the left."

Now that she was on the Baller, and in the company of old friends, maybe this *was* madness. They could chalk it up to two lone Jews bonding at a Christmas party, and go their separate ways. Stay at opposite ends of the boat for the duration of the ride.

Beck was cute, he'd find company in no time. And she'd end up in a cuddle fest by the end of the night with one of her Year Course guys as usual, like Avi or Jonah – guys safe to be herself with, no danger of hooking up. Just unconditional acceptance. No one she had to prove anything to.

Between the crowds, the lights and the interrogation, the heat was on. She barely felt the cold anymore. But now that she knew the price tag of her loaner jacket, she didn't dare take it off. Besides, it smelled like Beck, which wasn't the worst thing in the world.

She liked the novelty of it. Getting to know someone new. Maybe someone she'd *want* to open up to.

"So Beck is a nice, *rich* Jewish boy? Ruth Ruben would be beside herself." Avi grinned.

"New pact. Let's not talk about my mother tonight."

"*Bubbaleh...*" Jay did a damn good impression of her mother's Upper West Side accent. "It's just as easy to fall in love with a rich man..."

"And do you know how easy it would be to tip you off that ladder and overboard?"

So what if Beck had good – and expensive – taste for a Bridge & Tunnel guy? He didn't have Manhattan rent to pay or thirty-dollar take-out lunch salads to buy. Nora knew it was snobby of her, but she'd lived in Manhattan all her life. She couldn't imagine having such a city at your fingertips and living just outside its limits. It would be like...like looking into a snow globe all the time, and never getting to fully experience the magic inside.

"Go. Have fun. I'll come find you later," Talia squeezed Nora's arm. "After I feed the tired, poor, huddled masses yearning to break free."

Given that the boat full of mostly well-dressed Jews was about to cruise past the Statue of Liberty, it was ironically fitting.

"Speaking of suits..." Avi flicked Jonah's collar. "How many black light posters did you have to kill to make this horror, guy?"

"Hey, just 'cuz you look like a debonair, dead-sexy penguin doesn't give you the right to throw shade, dude." Jonah laughed and flipped the top hat Jay had donned for his emcee duties right off his head. "I'd look like a DC comic book villain if I dressed like you players."

Nora tuned out the guys' heckling. Maybe Beck ran the suburban field office? Maybe he was Hedstrom's equal. She shivered at that thought. *Stop,* she mentally chastised herself. Beck had readily agreed not to talk shop tonight on her behest, so why was she stressing herself out with the intrusive thought loops?

Jay had called her a workaholic, but it was more than that. She tended to hyper-focus on things her whole life, and work just happened to be a big part of it.

It used to be something she enjoyed.

Alex had made his way to the west side of the top deck, but had refrained from joining the camera-phone-happy revelers snapping photos by the rail. Instead, he had taken a seat at one of the many pianos he'd spied on board. Instead of tip jars on top, boxes meant for *tzedakah* – voluntary charity collection – sat awaiting to be filled.

Jay had philanthropy down to a science, using art.

Des Moines had dozens of public pianos across town – street pianos placed by the Iowa Arts Council – and Alex had probably played every one of them. But a yacht piano?

Challenge accepted.

Soft notes were lost to the sea air, but when Alex alternated with forte, the sound began to draw people. The hush crumple of bills and clinking of coins could be heard as people came closer to show their appreciation via charitable donation.

Sometimes even he marveled at the stroke of his fingers on the keys, always finding ways to coax such powerful chords. He knew there was a brain-body connection, but his brain wasn't always thinking such nice things about himself.

People began to clap, drifting away as he dwindled down Leonard Cohen's most celebrated song.

"That's beautiful, Beck."

He turned to find Nora, his blazer folded over her bare arm.

"Thanks." He was no Buckley channeling Cale channeling Cohen, but he made his own personal *Hallelujah* each time he played it. "Twenty-five years of playing."

Nora sat on the bench next to him. "I never got past *Twinkle, Twinkle Little Star*."

"I can teach you *Mary Had a Little Lamb*," he teased. "That's what usually comes next." She gave him a jostle with her shoulder, then reached for the long overdue cocktail he'd left on the top of the piano.

"Trust me, it's better now that the ice has melted."

She laughed. "Jay insists on Jedi Masters tending bar every year." Taking a sip, she winced. "Yep. The booze is strong with this one."

Others were waiting to play, so they relinquished their seat.

"Do you want to get a closer look at Lady Liberty?"

"Methinks the bar has already been set by a lady in a dress tonight."

"Yeah, but that one is clearly carrying a torch for you," she teased, tossing his jacket to him.

"Touché." He slipped it on before staggering a step back, feigning a mortal blow to his ego. Together they strolled ever farther away from the crowd, toward the back of the boat. *The stern? The prow?* Alex had lived landlocked his whole life in Des Moines; the nautical terms escaped him.

Nora, on the other hand, resided on an island – and an exotic one at that. Never more clear than now, as the lights of lower Manhattan winked at them. It reminded Alex of countless iconic movie opening shots, full of promise – of adventure and opportunity awaiting.

"I never tire of this view." Nora gripped the rail and took in a breath of crisp, night air.

"Would you mind...grabbing a pic?"

Glancing over her shoulder at him, she made her request, voice suddenly shy. "My mom will guilt trip me all the way into Passover if I don't document this moment for her." She swept her hand down, from bodice to bow.

"Not at all."

The lights of the skyline hugged her curves, competing for attention. He snapped several before handing her his phone so she could text them to herself. The modern day way of asking for a girl's number without really asking.

"Did you find your friend?"

"I did. Did you ditch your cousin?"

An unspoken agreement seemed to pass between them.

If either had needed an excuse to beg off, to go hang with their own social crowd – Nora's apparently included rock stars like Avi freaking Wolfson, of all people – they were free to go if they chose.

"Did the requisite shot with Drew and...done for the night." Alex chuckled. "Family obligations over."

Ha, right. If only.

Something about the night air made him want to share his whole sordid tale with her. He wasn't normally one to hold back. But maybe it was staring down into the darkness below them that kept him from telling her – you only knew the water was there from its gentle, persistent lapping.

Or perhaps it was how she wound her arm through his, pulling him close until their cheeks touched and they both fit in the frame. Her finger on the button of his camera app, capturing the two of them against that surreal backdrop. And capturing their night together.

Full of promise.

Opportunity awaiting.

Chapter Six

As the boat wound under the Brooklyn and Manhattan Bridges and uptown toward the calmer waters of the Hudson, Nora played tour guide, pointing out various landmarks and buildings, and answering his questions with questions of her own.

"Yankees or Mets?" she asked, as they approached the famed stadium of the Bronx Bombers, its circles of light vaguely reminiscent of a grounded UFO from their vantage point. "Since baseball was your Bar Mitzvah theme..."

"Neither." He smiled. "Cubbies, all the way."

"I know very little about baseball, so I am not offended. But you might not want to say that too loud on a boat full of drunken New Yorkers."

Beck laughed. "My grandfather got his start selling peanuts at the Chicago home games. He taught me everything he knew. Or should I say, he could explain everything in life in terms of how it related to baseball. Loyalty and where it lies. How to spot your rival, and what to do about them. Although, I was born after the rivalry died down between the Mets and Cubs, when they ended up in different divisions."

He turned back to the lights of the stadium, leaning on the railing. "My grandpa would've loved this. I lost him earlier this fall."

She rolled her hand over his, felt his grasp on the bar tighten. "I'm sorry. I know...same with my grandma, this past April. The feeling just sucks, right?"

Beck turned to face her. "And everyone always says that thing, when you lose someone, about their memory. May it be for a blessing. But..."

"I know...it doesn't feel like we get nearly enough time with them to make all the memories."

"Exactly." His grip loosened, allowing her fingers to thread through his.

"My best memory will always stand out, though. My grandma taking me to my first Broadway show. It was *The Lion King* at the New Amsterdam Theatre."

Beck shifted so his back shielded her from the wind, his body accommodating hers as she leaned in for warmth. "That's the oldest operating theater on Broadway, isn't it?"

"Impressive, Beckman." She smiled. "I was eight, finally the age to make the pilgrimage with Bubbe. We dressed up. The show, of course, was amazing, in all its dramatic, sweeping theatrical glory. But intermission? That was truly magical to a little girl with a sweet tooth and a touch of ADHD."

She could still recall the house lights, bringing everyone out of their spell. The opulence of the lobby, its red velvet and gold. Tuxedoed men and women, popping wine corks, popping corn, their glass counters full of treats to be enjoyed until the lights flashed. How even the labels on the treats were displayed in perfect symmetry. She shared all this with Beck. "I was hooked."

"Is that what drew you to concessions?"

She gave him a warning look, to which he quickly added, "Origin stories don't count as shop talk."

That was true, and it did feel good to recall those early days. "It felt like...a family. In the best house in town. So, yes – working concessions was my first job in high school, and then I interned in wardrobe shops for a few of the theaters during college – costume design major."

Beck's eyes widened. "On Broadway?"

"Yep." She had a several draping credits to her name to prove it, too. "I was a swing dresser, meaning I would work on several different shows at once."

Nora had loved the flurry of controlled chaos that came with the job, helping keep the shows on track and running smoothly, with the audience none the wiser as to all that had to happen backstage to achieve that.

"It always seems like magic to me," Beck said, as if reading her thoughts. "How fast the actors are able to transform from one look to another. Especially such intricate costumes. In any show, much less a Broadway production, wow. You must know a lot of trade secrets."

"Magnets, zippers and Velcro." Nora laughed. "I could also bore you on the merits of trucker's hitch knots and Whopper Poppers."

"Not boring at all, in fact... I'd say it's all pretty *fastenating*." He gave her a nudge, goading her to laugh again.

"Go ahead, say your worst. You wouldn't believe how many pick-up lines revolve around 'how fast can you undress me?' once guys find out you do that for a living."

Beck cringed. "I'm not going to apologize on behalf of

guys everywhere, but...that's some aged Wisconsin cheese right there. We really need to step up our game."

Nora hadn't spoken about that part of her life in a while, but the thought of it was bittersweet. Costuming was a competitive industry and its coveted, full-time jobs were basically non-existent. And depending on "day work" – things like stitching, shoe calls, hat calls, beading calls – to supplement evening show gigs in order to pay the rent had been exhilarating but exhausting.

She had meant for her move to Britesmith's corporate office to be temporary after graduating, but somehow six years had gone by. Although the hours were better than backstage, and she could once again be in the audience and enjoy the shows, she knew it wasn't her true calling.

What would her grandmother say, if she knew how far Nora had strayed off the path? Bubbe had been a trailblazer herself – she had been in the Radio City Rockettes in the '70s, and had been instrumental in saving Radio City from the wrecking ball.

Her mantra to her granddaughter had always been to *be true to yourself, love what you do, and do the best job you can.*

Up until today, Nora had been doing the best she could. But as the last straw had given way at the office party, she realized she had sacrificed the other two in the process.

Before her thoughts veered further into dangerous waters, Beck wrapped his other arm around her. "Speaking of cheese...how about finding some of that food your friend is famous for?"

"Oh, you have no idea what you're in for."

Nora wasn't kidding, Alex soon discovered. New York Jews did not mess around when it came to food, its proportions or its variety. Every level of the boat boasted a different culinary delight, with distinctions for every dietary restriction, religious or otherwise. The buffet tables groaned with a variety of dishes, from seasonal Hanukkah favorites to quintessential New York all-year-round traditions.

Alex didn't know where to start first, what to try next. He followed Nora's lead, loading plates of bite-sized items they could stroll with to the next area.

Sections were designed for maximum grazing and minimal lines. Groupings of tables were available if you wanted to nosh and socialize, never too far from the action. There were other bars, too – not just serving the specialty Hanukkah cocktails, which they had doubled back to for a refill, but wine, beer, non-alcoholic juicery options and even an egg cream bar.

"Is that a matzo ball soup station?"

Alex thought he had seen everything, but people were walking by with glass teacup-sized samplings with the fluffiest matzo balls he had ever seen bobbing on top, and well...he had to try.

But not before Nora pushed something past his lips that tasted all at once like home and heaven. Under the perfect golden fried layer was a delicate pasta that practically melted on the tongue, followed by a zing of cinnamon, sweet cheese and the tiniest crunch of apples. "It came to Talia in a dream," she explained. "Fried Kugel Ravioli. Good, right?"

"Put it this way. If a plate of these fell overboard, my cousin Drew was drowning, and there was only one life preserver..." He laughed at his own dumb analogy, and the imagery of a plate of kugel bobbing in the East River.

Warmed by the food now filling their bellies, they ventured back out onto one of the heated decks. Just as Nora had pointed out famous landmarks, she began discretely pointing out celebrity passengers, squeezing his arm each time as they walked by.

"The Matzo Baller is infamous for a lot of things, but one of the coolest is the impromptu 'sessions' that might happen, given the guest list," she explained. "You just never know who is climbing on board with you. That's why no two Ballers are ever the same."

They ducked back into the ballroom in time to catch a stand-up bit by an up-and-coming comedienne Alex had recently seen on a streaming special, and a karaoke performance by an actor known for a singular superhero role, who brought an impressive "One Day" by Matisyahu in the back lounge. It didn't seem to matter if they had three or one-hundred-and-three people watching them, it was just part of the night's fun.

"How long has Jay been doing this?" Alex marveled, stuffing some of the larger bills he carried into one of the many *tzedakah* boxes near the talent. "He makes it look so effortless."

"Six years of actual cruises, but it grew out of his desire to gather all eight of us together once a year, after we got back from Israel. That's been the hardest part, sadly. Like herding stray cats."

A flurry of activity across the room caught her eye. Catering staff were rolling out carts of desserts that looked as height-defying as the champagne tower. A redhead in a chef's coat was directing them. "We're all well-fed strays, at least," she murmured. "Talia ensures that."

Sure enough, a tray was set within their reach by a

young waiter. "Sufganiyot Croquembouche," the kid pronounced slowly, "with sour cherry cream."

"If you mean fried donuts fused together by caramel, I am all for it." Nora wiggled the top donut off the pile, and then a second one, sending a sprinkling of powdered sugar down her arm. The rest of the tower stayed intact, its structure bolstered by maraschino cherries filling in the holes and a halo of spun caramel candy floss. But Alex had the feeling the tower would soon be breached, as more party guests descended.

"Not the ideal first date food." She gasped a laugh after a perfect swirl of jelly and pastry cream rocketed out as she bit down. Alex decided to conquer his in one bite, making her laugh even harder. "We've come a long way since Maureen from the Sales department's yule log." She clapped her hand over her mouth. "Origin stories AND office party dessert fails don't count as shop talk, agreed?"

"Depends...does this count as a first date, Ruben?" He arched a brow at her.

"What happens on the Baller, stays on the Baller, Beckman. And seeing as I lured you on here with my all-access pass..."

Her grin absolutely untethered him. There was definitely something about being out to sea that made anything happening on the mainland seem very far away in comparison.

They checked out the lower cabin areas, where Jay was engaged in what appeared to be a high-limit table game of dreidel. Ladies hung off his powder-blue tux, like they were on a casino floor in Vegas. Shouts and cheers erupted.

"Jews and gentiles, he rose out of JCC basement tournaments to take the title of two-time Major League Dreidel champion of the WORLD!"

"That's our friend Jonah," Nora explained, pointing out a tall guy in a loud-patterned suit who was making it rain, gelt-style. "He's from New Jersey. Or as he would say: New *Jewsey*. Total mensch. He comes every year without fail."

"And Avi Wolfson?"

Alex hadn't glimpsed the singer again since his appearance during the candle lighting. But the embrace Nora and the others had shared with him definitely signified he was within their inner circle and they in his.

"Twenty gelt coins says Baltimore's boy wonder will be crooning into a mic by the end of the night," Nora smiled. "Even on Shabbat, Avi can't stay too idle for too long."

They settled on one of the low leather couches lining the perimeter of the cabin. Open windows above their heads brought in cool breezes from the lower deck, and it was dimly lit, set back from the side of the room where the games were going on.

"You like to make bets, don't you, Ruben?"

"A pact is different from a bet, Beckman. But if you want to add stakes to make it more appealing..."

"I already find you very, very appealing, Nora."

Maybe it was the way he said her name, or the way they'd opened up their vulnerable sides on the deck, talking about their dreams and their losses. Or even the unabashed stuff-your-face Jewish food fest where he matched her, knish-for-kneidlach, and still had the appetite to try more.

She felt like she had known Beck far longer in that comfortable way, yet – there was something that excited her, the newness of his mouth and how it reacted to her kiss. The solidness of his biceps, his chest, as her hands explored.

The feel of his long, strong fingers in her hair, gently tracing circles behind her earlobes.

His dark eyes, taking the time to watch, like hers did. To marvel.

Making out with a co-worker. On a party boat. In a ball gown. Twenty feet away from two of her best male friends. All of this should've been enough to make her want to run, Cinderella-style, at the stroke of midnight.

But all she could think of was *two more hours*.

Two more hours till the boat docked and they could steal away somewhere without an audience. At least the couches were low and cozy, the lighting discrete. Nora didn't dare look, but assumed there were other couples up to similar mischief around them. The moonlight setting and all, and each part of the boat a different mood.

The dreidel game had dwindled down, leaving the floor free for the disco ball above to slowly shine its spots. It cast patterns across their entwined legs, then up Beck's torso to where her fingers had loosened his tie. She liked the way it played across his jawline as he tilted his head to kiss the crook of her elbow. *Hello, new erogenous zone*, her lady parts zinged.

"Still good?" His murmur against her skin gave her the best kind of chills.

"Still great," she whispered.

Beck's mouth captured hers again, his tongue sweet with the taste of powdered sugar. She could happily spend the next two hours like this, with this man worshipping parts of her that had gone unconsidered for a very long time.

What happens on the Baller, stays on the Baller.

Still, she wanted off the boat. She wanted to find out what would happen next.

"Naaaaarahhhh!"

Arms jangling with silver bracelets and mala beads swooped in first, followed by the scent of sweet orange and patchouli.

Sylvie Shapiro happened next, apparently.

"Haven't seen you in faaaaaevahhhh!" Sylvie made hugging an art, her limber frame collapsing onto the couch cushion next to them and molding itself to Nora's free side. Whether it was the Negev in summer or the five boroughs in December, Sylvie dressed in layers as light as gossamer, as if spun by silkworms and blessed by fairy dust. Or as Avi liked to call it, Burning Man aesthetic.

"Hi Sylvie, happy Hanukkah." Half-tangled in Beck, half now glued to Sylvie, all Nora could do was pat-pat her friend's floaty garment and long, blonde balayage hair in greeting.

It wasn't that Sylvie couldn't read a room – she just loved intimacy in all its forms and had no qualms about approaching any situation with open arms.

"This is Beck. Beck – my friend Sylvie."

Only two things grounded Sylvie: her ever-present combat boots and the Nikon hanging around her neck. Nora felt both as Sylvie leaned over to kiss Beck on both cheeks, her legs twining with theirs. "So I heard." She beamed. "Hi Beck!"

"Ope!" He stilled the swinging camera before it could do more damage. "Nice to meet you."

"You're not from around here, are you?"

Funny, coming from the girl they would tease on Year Course, about how her "Boston was showing" every time she got excited, upset or drunk.

She squeezed each of their legs goodbye and hopped up without waiting for a reply.

"You take good care of each other. I'm going to shoot Avi."

"I hope she means with her camera," Beck said after she was out of earshot.

Nora laughed. "Sylvie's mostly harmless." But not clueless, it was important to note; Jay or Talia could've easily sent Sylvie in to size Beck up. A stealth Cupid spy, her empathy keen to any vibes he may be laying down. "And yes, she's pretty much Avi's personal photographer. Mutual muses, those two."

Beck's splayed hand finger-counted against her thigh. "We're up to six. Of your eight friends from your gap year. Are the other two on the boat?"

Nora liked his hands-on math skills. She'd be fine if he added, subtracted, multiplied and divided against her body all the way back to the dock. And she'd happily tell him about Libby, the final of her fab four girl group. But the last integer of their Jew Crew?

Eli Gold.

Like an integer, he was positive and negative. Yet whole. A thing complete in itself.

Eli had the power to make all of her problems at work disappear with one phone call. Nora knew this. Yet...

Yet.

"Libby's my roommate, actually – but is spending the holiday with family because she leaves New York right after New Year's for Switzerland." As desperately as Nora needed to find a replacement to help with rent, there was truly no replacing Libby Sugarman. While they hadn't been as instantly close as she and Talia, their personalities – and their pitiful salaries – were perfectly suited for sharing five hundred and fifty square feet of Hell's Kitchen. But Nora couldn't fault her friend for jumping at the chance to study under a master chocolatier for a year.

Eli's doing, no doubt.

Nora was sure he had a few Swiss contacts, not to mention a few Swiss bank accounts.

Leap and the net will appear.

That was the last thing she heard from him, a week ago, via IsraelPost. Who takes the trouble to write one sentence, find a stamp, and airmail it across the world?

Eli, apparently.

If she needed that kind of advice, she could go buy a greeting card at the corner store. Because she *had* confided in him. About Britesmith. And he had totally let her down.

"Maybe next year," Nora said, which to her ears sounded just as disingenuous as uttering "Next year in Jerusalem" after Passover Seder. "There's always next year for all eight of us."

Chapter Seven

If anyone had told him, as he boarded his plane at DSM that morning for New York, that he'd be ending the day licking sugar off the arm of someone like Nora Ruben, he'd have thought they were out of their goddamn mind.

Now, Alex wondered if he had lost his.

This is a business trip. For your family business.

She is technically your employee.

He'd never believed in angels or devils on his shoulders before tonight, but they had apparently boarded the boat with him.

Not if I walk away from Myers and Sons.

In all fairness, it was something he had thought about doing before he even knew of Nora's existence.

Just tell her.

She'd had a bad workday and didn't want to talk about it.

So what? You've had a bad year.

Well, Nora was doing a pretty good job pushing that thought of out his head. They had managed to find their way back to what they had been doing before her friend had interrupted them.

You're not from around here.

Her friend Sylvie's observation mixed with his dueling conscience. As did her parting words: To take good care of each other.

Just give us this one night.

He didn't know if he was asking this of the angel, the devil, Grandpa My *Z"L*, his Uncle Marty, or Nora herself.

Nora, who was on the verge of letting him pull that bow and unwrap her like the best Hanukkah gift.

One night, that's all I'm asking.

"You probably have a train to catch," she started, "when we dock."

Had he voiced that out loud?

"A bridge to cross," She sighed against his mouth. "Or a tunnel –"

"Nora. I have a hotel room."

The boat began to slow and turn. Nora glimpsed the hulking mass of the USS Intrepid, the floating Sea, Air & Space Museum, docked a few piers up from where the Baller would finish its journey. Pretty soon, Jay's voice would come floating over the boat's intercom, thanking everyone for coming.

Passengers would pass back through the ballroom, providing one last chance to give *tzedakah,* bid goodbye to friends, and witness the final performance of the night – which was usually big and unannounced.

Avi's voice began to flow through the speakers. Even through a metal box, you could hear his star shine.

Nora took Beck's hand as they threaded through throngs of people still trying to get one last drink on, one last selfie as the boat rapidly approached the lights of Manhattan's west side. She knew this boat like the back of her hand after six years, and she knew they could pass through the kitchen to get to the ballroom quickly and, from there, she knew the way to a much less-utilized service ramp off the boat.

Talia's kitchen station was empty, lit only by utility lights and clean as a whistle. No one would've suspected the miracles she and her workers had performed out of the small galley space that night.

In the ballroom, passengers fell into two groups: those getting a second wind and making plans to hit a club or bar to prolong the magic until at least four a.m., and those on their last legs, relieved to sit for a few minutes and be entertained by Avi and the talented skeleton crew of musicians he had rounded up to perform the final song of the night.

"Wow." Beck drew a breath as they stopped to watch. "I've never caught a Painted Doors show live, but have heard great things. He's really talented."

Avi was mesmerizing, actually. His voice never failed to stop Nora in her tracks. She could be in the middle of Whole Foods, bag of Pirate Booty in her hands and grinning like a fool. Or reduced to tears in her hair salon. His originals were what put him on the map for mainstream consumption.

But when he did a cover song it was like a love letter in a bottle, from a time back when they all lived together in their own little desert oasis – full of mirages and miracles.

The Gen Z friend group all knew radio hits from the '60s, '70s and '80s, thanks to the dad of one of the host families from their *moshav*. Modi had been a DJ and claimed he taught his kids English from all the bands dominating the '80s airwaves. Especially those British and American rock bands that Avi seemed to easily chameleon into for his closest friends' amusement.

He used to do it to make them laugh through their farm chores; tie a bandana around his sweaty brow and be Axl Rose for an afternoon. He disrupted many an *Ulpan* class meant to improve their Hebrew with his renditions of Pink Floyd's "Another Brick in the Wall," claiming they needed no education. And he could play just about any of their requests on the battered acoustic guitar he brought with him while visiting them on the *kibbutzim* after some of their group was sent north.

And now he was singing a Bad Co. ballad based on three little colors: "Silver, Blue and Gold." Seemingly perfect for the Hanukkah holiday, but really a love and loss song, equally haunting and hopeful.

Avi gripped the mic with both hands. Somewhere along the cruise route he had shed his tux jacket. Lost his bow tie. With sleeves messily rolled above his tattoos and one shirt tail untucked, the singer looked like he'd either had a rough night at sea, or a roll in the hull with an adoring fan.

His curls were a disheveled cascade over one eye as he crooned, until he pushed through them with ringed fingers, smoothing them back. Cradling his head as if it were too heavy to bear while aiming lyrics like an arrow to the bullseye in the crowd.

He didn't even have to look to hit his target.

Sylvie's face was hidden behind her camera lens, giving nothing away. Her golden tresses like a curtain on either side. For someone who practically floated through life, she channeled intense focus as she leaned back, then forward. Snapping shot after shot of her subject.

Nora scanned the room for the others. Jay was in what looked like intense talks with some of the uniformed crew, but his easy grin broke out here and there, confirming the success of the night.

Talia, surprisingly, was nowhere in sight. Nora felt a pang of regret that she had missed a rare moment to spend with her friend once the food service had wrapped up.

The Hanukkah-themed cocktail bar near the pillar where she and Beck had shared a kiss was roped off, looking like it had been sold out for hours. Jonah leaned back with large elbows against it, watching the crowd. Nora waited until he caught sight of her.

"Give me a minute?" Her request delivered to Beck's ear on her tiptoes, so she could be heard over the swelling song, but also an excuse for her lips to brush that scruff on his cheek as he nodded.

Jonah unclipped the velvet rope for her to join him at the empty bar. She scooted in and gave him a hug. "Don't hate me, but I'm doing the Irish goodbye thing."

He belly-laughed. For someone who actually had a quarter-Irish in him, Jonah was never the first to leave a party, and always made sure he said goodbye to everyone at least twice.

"You good, though? Of sound mind and bod to leave with...nice suit guy?"

"Yeah, it's good. I'm good." She didn't feel she needed his consent or approval, but she was glad to check in with at least one of her crew before leaving the boat.

"I'm just surprised, Nor...you hooking up with a co-worker. Especially since work has been such a Jocko on your back lately." He quickly traced a triangle across the front of his black velvet jacket, followed by an upside down one to make a hexagram – like crossing himself, only with a

Star of David. "Jocko of Blessed Memory," he added, as always, before palming something from his big bear paw into her hand.

"Just in case, times two."

"These better not glow in the dark like your suit." She discreetly slid the condoms into her clutch.

Jonah's brows raised behind his hornrims. "Million-dollar idea."

She snorted. "Yeah, let's get Eli to invest."

"I'm sure he'd be in for the seed round." He grinned.

Nora gave him a push. "Goodbye, love you, call you tomorrow."

"It *is* tomorrow, fool."

Leaving mid-song, combined with Nora's knowledge of a back exit and Alex calling the Town Car ahead, helped them beat the crowd. "Wow, that's novel," Nora marveled as he ushered her away from the mess of taillights crowding the Uber and taxi zones. "I thought car services were extinct these days."

It was the same company Britesmith had sent to fetch him at the airport; same driver and everything. But Alex made sure it was on his personal credit card this time.

"Good to see you again, Mr. Beckman. I delivered your bags to the hotel earlier."

The driver provided bottles of water and even a phone charger, which Nora gratefully accepted as they glided across town.

Alex noted the abundance of white lights, twinkling across restaurant awnings and framing countless apartment windows. He wondered if New York was this magical at two a.m. all year round, or just during the holidays. People were still out on the streets, despite the cold temps and the late hour.

"Look," Nora whispered, leaning across him. She pointed out the window. The Empire State Building illuminated Manhattan with white and blue lights, and a flickering "candle" antenna. "That's for us."

He kissed her forehead. The Town Car was warm, and way more shock-absorbing than that earlier taxi ride. As revved up as they had both been on that couch earlier, the spell woven was giving way to sleep...and he had no issues with that. Waking up next to this beauty, and prolonging that magic...

"To think I'd be getting up in a few hours to head into the office," she yawned, laughing to herself. "That I had even considered preparing for Team Hayseed's visit possibly worth the overtime..."

There was that knot in the pit of his stomach again. "Nora –"

"Oh, shit. I broke the pact, didn't I?"

No, she had broken the spell.

Honoring her kibosh on work talk had been both a blessing and a curse, but now he was damned if he did or didn't.

Before he could form the words, she sat up and turned to face him. "Beck, listen. I have to be honest with you – as much as I seemed spontaneous tonight, I'm not. I am methodical, work-obsessed and, well... I've never had a one-night stand in my life."

Her self-depreciating laugh twisted his insides. "I just – well, for one night, I wanted things to be different. I wanted not to care. To be like the other girls in the office who seem to be able to shut off their brain so easily at five pm. And who come in Monday morning with an epic story. But the truth is, even if we were to have an incredible night together… I probably still *will* go into the office tomorrow… which is today, but whatever. What I mean is, the fantasy would end. And if that's disappointing or a turn-off –"

Alex took her hands in his. "Are you kidding? Nora, your brain and how you tick – *that's* a turn-on. Tightly wound or not. And believe me when I say this entire time with you has been epic…"

As much as the night had turned out to exceed his expectations, and as much as he wanted it to continue, he couldn't let her think they were just co-workers.

And the heartbreaking part of it was they could never be anything else, either – not as long as he was following his uncle's orders or honoring his grandfather's wishes.

I've done things I'm not proud of.

Whatever Nora was covering up for her boss…Alex couldn't use their connection as an excuse to deny it, or as a way to find out.

"But as much as I may live to regret this…the night has to end here. Because I don't want you walking into the office Monday morning feeling any worse about work than you do right now."

He felt her stiffen in his arms, pulling out of his embrace. Shock had replaced all sleepiness, and confusion crossed her face.

"I should've told you the minute we met. I'm…"

"Say it. You're married, you asshole."

"No. Worse."

On a scale of jackass to asshole…"I'm Team Hayseed."

And I'm here to fire you.

He wasn't going to say that, because he knew – he'd known the minute she walked out of that party – she did not belong on his uncle's list. He didn't know the how or the why, but he was determined to get to the bottom of whatever was going on in that Manhattan office.

And come Monday morning, she would know that, too.

But anything between them – between now and then – would seriously complicate things.

He tapped the driver's shoulder. "Take her wherever she wants to go," he said as the car stopped for a red light. Before Nora could react or he could change his mind, Alex reached for the door handle.

Chapter Eight

"Lady...you gotta make a decision here."

The driver gestured for the honking gridlock behind him to go around. He couldn't very well move while Nora stood in traffic, watching Beck cut through Bryant Park.

"Are you fucking kidding me?"

She had become one of *those* people, yelling swear words on 42nd Street after midnight. Cursing her heels, cursing the universe. "Can you just – " she pulled the skirt of her dress around her legs as she climbed back into the car, " – follow him or cut him off on the next block?"

"No can do, miss. Sixth Avenue runs uptown."

For some reason, this infuriated her more than being abandoned in the middle of Midtown. "You think I don't know that? I've lived here my whole damn life!"

"Whaddaya want, me to drive across the ice rink? Through the library building? I'll have to cut across to Madison and go up around the block to get back to Fifth."

"We'll lose him in the time that takes!"

"Look." He softened his tone. "I got a daughter your

age. No guy is worth chasing. And nothing good happens after two a.m. So let me drop you home, sweetheart."

Nora flopped back against the leather seat.

"You said you dropped his bags earlier. Where?"

Steely blue eyes, bracketed by the kind of wizened wrinkles her dad's had, glimpsed her in the rearview mirror. "Honey, if you don't even know where he was – "

"From," she said calmly. "Where from?"

"I picked him up at LaGuardia."

No bridge. No tunnel.

Beck really was Team Hayseed.

"Okay." Nora closed her eyes, refusing to let the tears fall. "Okay," she whispered again. "Turn here, 47th please. Corner of 9th is fine. Thanks."

Of course he was. Even Sylvie had picked up on it.

Not from around here.

Jay and Avi's words echoed in her ears as well.

What's he want...what's he expecting...

Her phone, now fully charged, lit up with a message. As if on cue, Sylvie had sent a group text, one image.

Happy Hanukkah to the OG Matzo Ballers!

How she had snapped a photo of all six of them on the boat without them knowing was pure Sylvie. She must've talked her way up to the deck of the captain's bridge, because she was above everything, even the menorah. In the foreground, in selfie stance, flashing a peace sign.

There was Jay on the ladder in the background, mic held aloft and candles softly glowing, and the four others below, holding the ladder. It wasn't the clearest photo, given the sunset and distance, but it stirred a storm of emotions, especially as one by one, the reactions started to ping.

Libby's heart showed up first, followed by one from Jonah. Jay dropped the double exclamation points while Avi threw the rock horns. Nora pushed her own keyboard on auto-pilot, tears blurring the heart she shared. Eli's jinxed hers, arriving at the exact same time and making her smile, despite everything.

Talia's reaction had yet to appear in the chat, but Nora was too exhausted to wait for it. Hopefully her friend's evening had turned out better than her own flaming shit show. She shut off her phone, ready to be done with this day, this night, this dress...this Hanukkah.

Team Hayseed.

Alex peered thirty-six stories down. The view from his room was spectacular, the minibar impressively stocked. His luggage had been stowed in the corner and turn-down service had occurred, down to the imported chocolates waiting on the pillow.

It was exactly what he had wanted upon arrival in New York, fourteen hours earlier.

Now, he wanted to punch a hole through the wall.

Coward.

His phone's GPS had led him to the hotel, but he hadn't remembered his feet making the trek. He hadn't noticed the cold; a numbness had set in.

No. The numbness had *returned.* How he had felt since losing his grandfather. Today, with Nora, had been the first time in a long time he had actually felt things – good things – and not just due to their chemistry.

He flopped back on the bed, fully clothed.

Something jingled.

Reaching into the pocket of his suit jacket, he came out with the lone jingle bell. She must've slid it in there, after he'd loaned her his coat.

It hadn't just been how incredibly attracted he was to her. It was getting a glimpse at a day in the life of Nora Ruben. Not just some name on a list.

He had been along for the ride – literally. Seeing the love she had for her friends, the pride she had in her faith. He had no idea what she did for Britesmith – but he'd bet she'd loved it, too, once upon a time.

She was an integral part of the New York office. He had sensed it in Hedstrom's introduction, in the way she carried herself in front of her co-workers.

He had arrived focused on the New York 54.

Now his focus had narrowed down to one.

He could hear the muted traffic below, the occasional whoop of a siren breaking through the white noise.

Protect New York, Alexi.

He didn't know if Nora could help or harm his mission.

His heart was a whole other matter.

Chapter Nine

Alex had fallen asleep on top of the bedcovers, suit and all. The tie Nora had perfectly loosened with flirty fingers last night had wrapped like a noose around his neck during his slumber. Pretty fitting.

He smelled like latke grease and her perfume. It was pure torture.

Stripping to his boxers and undershirt, he called the concierge to inquire about dry cleaning. "Of course, sir. The Langham prides itself on express service, we'll have it back to you before start of business, Monday morning."

Monday morning – *fuck my life*, Alex thought as he crammed his suit, tie and all, into the cloth laundry bag provided by the hotel for hanging on the door. Start of business, end of business; he no longer cared.

Nora stood in the doorway, fist about to knock.

The first thing Alex noticed was how tiny she was. Not April in the goth gear from the office party, tiny. But in running shoes, not heels, in leggings and a puffer jacket rather than formal dress, and with her hair piled in a messy bun on top of her head? Tiny and still traffic-stopping cute.

The second thing he noticed was the pungent aroma coming from the bag in her other hand.

"How – ?"

"How did I find you? I channeled my inner narcissistic asshole and asked myself: Where would I hang my three-thousand-dollar suits? Naturally, a thousand-dollar-a-night five-star hotel on the east side," she snarked. "Plus your driver took pity on me."

Tiny, but certainly not diminished. Her New York accent sounded stronger, too.

"I was going to ask how you slept. And *suit*. Singular." He held up the laundry bag, still in his hand. "Plus that dress of yours hardly looked thrift store."

"Rented. Not owned. And poorly."

Her face now scrubbed free of makeup, Alex noticed slight olive-toned circles under her eyes. He wondered if they were hereditary or from lack of quality sleep.

"What's in the bag?" he asked.

"I'm assuming you've never tried an authentic New York City bagel." She passed it over the threshold. "Hand-rolled and kettle-boiled. There's an everything with white-fish, and a poppy with dill and lox spread."

"So essentially the smelliest combination you could think of."

"Yep." If a smile could be both sweet and sarcastic, she flashed it. "No chance of kissing someone with garlic, onion and smoked fish breath. And poppy seeds in their teeth."

"Well, there's also no mistletoe hanging in my doorway, so you're safe to stand under it all day. Or you could come in for a cup of coffee."

He moved aside and let her make her choice.

Boxers, bedhead...thank God I brought reinforcements.

Nora had sifted through every scenario, and every stage of emotion as she unsuccessfully tried for sleep in the few hours she had been home. She'd shifted blame and anger and guilt and shame between the both of them. He should've told her who he was. She should've let him. He'd tried to bring up work – but he had also tried to get into her pants. Were either a genuine desire or just a ploy? A power play?

"I shouldn't have called you – or anyone from Iowa – a hayseed." She was truly sorry about that.

"That's not why I left you last night."

Ouch. She deserved that.

He massaged the back of his neck slowly, staring at her as he did so. She couldn't help notice how his triceps strained against the thin white sleeve of his T. Definitely not something she'd noticed about "nice suit guy" yesterday.

She realized how little she knew about him. She'd made him into what she had wanted him to be last night. And now she was realizing her mistake.

"Why don't you brew us some coffee while I hop in the shower." He gestured toward the Nespresso machine on the counter near the wet bar before padding out of sight.

A moment later, she heard the hiss of water. She wondered if he, like she, did some of his best thinking in the shower.

And what he was currently thinking of her.

As Nora had washed away the confusion and humiliation this morning, a new resolve had set in. She had professionally entertained countless prospective clients, investors, and out-of-town colleagues while employed by Britesmith. Midtown was practically built for the perfect forty-five-minute business lunch, and she knew all the best places.

She'd also onboarded and oriented new employees, as well as conducted exit interviews under every situation with the utmost tact.

In the hospitality industry, she was a superstar. She could certainly be hospitable over the next forty-eight hours to Team...Iowa. And Monday? Come what may.

It was probably why Hedstrom had introduced them in the first place. Not because they were the only Jews in the room. No, her boss – as insufferable as he could be at times – knew her strong points. Her ability to handle just about every situation professionally.

So it was a boxers and bagels situation. *Keep your cool, Ruben.*

She shed her jacket, tightened her top-knot and got to work. The warm aroma of espresso filled the light-drenched room, whose cream walls and slate-gray curtains seemed to soak up the winter morning sun.

She kicked off her sneakers, sinking into the plush, snowy carpeting as she carried their steaming cups to the small table near the window. The view was familiar yet foreign at the same time: city streets she had traipsed her whole life, but rarely glimpsed from such a height. If she squinted far enough, she could almost see the rooftops of Talia's neighborhood.

Her best friend must've sensed a vibration in the universe, because Nora's phone lit up.

> I hope you are having as much fun as I am right now

The text was accompanied by a photo – the back view of a tall, built dude looking up at a menu board. Something told Nora he wasn't just some random stranger Talia had met in line at the bagel place.

For Tal to even be functioning before sundown after the feat she pulled off on the Baller was a miracle in itself. Much less out on a date?

Nora bit her lip, laughing. Her self-proclaimed "kitchen mouse" bestie had gone and caught herself a big ginger cat, from the looks of it. *Go, Talia.*

Her host was back. In jeans now, feet still bare. He wore a gray Drake University T-shirt and an open flannel, his dark hair slicked back. Two-day-old scruff looked even better on him than yesterday's.

Just an observation.

Not a reason to want to run her hand over its scratchy-soft surface to see if it was as sensory-soothing as a flip-sequin pillow.

He held out his hand. "Hi. I'm Alex Beckman. Son of Alice and Sam Beckman. Grandson of the late Leah and Hal Myers."

"Who got his start selling peanuts at the ballgames."

"Yep. The last son of the original Myers and Sons. Now run by *his* son – my Uncle Marty." He gestured around him. "This was his planned trip, originally. He booked this hotel. So technically, he's the narcissistic asshole."

"Sorry about that, as well." She was two for two. "Did he also buy you the suit?"

"Gimme a little credit." He dimpled in her direction, and she took that as a win. "It's my favorite – and my lucky one. Which is why I wore it on the plane. I hate flying. Any other questions?"

"Can I still call you Beck?"

"Yes." He unwrapped the bagels, pulling them apart where they were sliced in half so they could each sample both kinds of schmears. "Anything else?"

"And...there are Jews in Iowa?"

He laughed, covering his mouthful of whitefish salad. "Yes...we are a small but mighty one percent of the population." He washed it down with coffee, regarding her over the rim of his bistro mug.

"Can I ask *you* a question?"

She tensed, setting her bagel aside. "Shoot."

"What are we doing...after we consume this rocket fuel and breakfast of champions?"

Alex had seen bulletproof Nora at the work party, safety-in-numbers Nora with her Baller posse. Flirty Nora, evasive Nora when she hadn't really known who he was.

And slightly snarky Nora once she did.

What – who – else was he going to get today?

And was he ready for her?

"You can't come to New York during the holiday season and not get a tour from a lifelong New Yorker." She avoided his eyes, picking poppy seeds off the top of her half-eaten bagel with a rounded fingernail. "And cousin Drew showing you the inside of some boujee finance bro bar or his favorite strip club doesn't exactly count."

Hot damn. *Observant AF*.

"We'll be outside most of the day. So dress warmly and comfortably."

"No problem there." He gestured to his jeans. "This is me."

"And this is me." Nora sat lotus-style, stocking feet tucked under her on the chair. She'd shed her big down jacket, and her clavicles and curves were all covered in layers: black thermal Henley, oversized zipped hoodie. The

Chai necklace was the only familiar thing. Even her smile was different now. A bit more tentative.

It was unspoken. The pact may've been over, but a new test of some kind lingered.

One of trust, perhaps.

He thought of some of the things he told Nora last night, and wondered if she was thinking about them, too. What his grandfather had taught him.

About loyalty, and how to spot your rival.

He could practically hear his grandfather now.

Put the ball in play, Alexi.

"And after that?"

"We'll light the second candle at sundown. Because no one should be alone on Hanukkah."

Chapter Ten

It was always fun to see her city through fresh eyes. But Nora had to admit, Beck made it even more so.

They started by walking up Fifth Avenue. So much to see, especially during the holiday season. First and foremost, Patience and Fortitude, the library lions, decked out in their neck wreaths. December alone was usually reason enough for locals to avoid the area around Rockefeller Center. But a week before Christmas? Trying to get anywhere near the big tree, or the skating rink, was madness. Ditto with the iconic holiday window displays, necessitating velvet ropes and security guards.

But the city had wisely instituted a pedestrian-only thoroughfare for select weekends in December, allowing them to walk eleven of the busiest blocks up the middle of the vehicle-free road.

They strolled – *strolled!* – up Fifth from West 48th to 57th street, nothing short of a miracle. Frantic shoppers and harried tourists kept to the sidewalks, mostly. Beck seemed content to view it all from afar. "It's beautiful," he admitted.

"But even watching from the outskirts, kind of overwhelming."

Nora agreed.

Honestly, most of December felt like that to her as an adult. Too many gatherings and not enough weekends. Too many gifts to buy and not enough money. She secretly liked it best when Hanukkah fell earlier in the calendar year. Separate and not to be confused with – or consumed by – all the other seasonal merriment.

She told him stories of coming downtown as a kid, trips with her friends and their parents, even sitting on Santa's lap once in Macy's. Feeling like an imposter, at just seven years old, but still not turning down that free candy cane.

There was a time, Beck confided, where he, too, secretly believed in some magic he didn't quite understand, listening for the sound of reindeer hoofs on the rooftop. Wanting to share in the building excitement of his neighborhood friends, even though his was the only house on their block unadorned, come December.

"That's one of the things I enjoyed about the Matzo Baller. Hanukkah was really everywhere we looked. For once, a total immersion...not an afterthought."

Nora nodded. "Definitely Jay's intent, I think. Legit, right?"

They had arrived at the entrance to Central Park, one of the places Beck had mentioned he'd wanted to see before flying home on Tuesday. "Speaking of legit..."

A thirty-six foot tall menorah stood in Grand Army Plaza, making Jay's twelve-foot masterpiece at sea seem miniscule. Come sundown, Nora knew there would be crowds to rival the Rockefeller Plaza Christmas tree, clamoring to watch it illuminated. But in the light of day, the impressive structure was easy to walk right up to.

"Largest in the world...crafted by an Israeli sculptor," Beck read from the plaque nearby. Nora stealth-snapped a few photos of him, peering up at it, hands in his coat pockets. Thanks to the photos he had taken for her last night, she had his number to text him, too. "My mom will love these, thanks. She's a sculptor, too."

As they entered the park, the rest of the city fell away, save for a jutting skyscraper looming in the distance here and there. Beck seemed surprised to see snow covering some of the lawn. "We haven't had much yet this year," Nora supplied. "And traffic and pedestrians clear it pretty quick on the streets. But I love that there are parts untouched in here."

The path they were on dipped down and curved around, white surrounding them on either side. With the blue sky doming around them, Nora remembered the snow globe observation she had had last night. The thought that New York was somehow better, and those outside of it were missing out.

Back when she thought Beck was just a bridge or tunnel removed from it.

Thinking of him now, living his life across multiple state lines in the middle of the country...that left her feeling like maybe she had been the one missing out. And that if it weren't for Britesmith being acquired by Myers and Sons, they may have never met.

They wound through Nora's favorite parts of the park, past Wollman Rink and the Carousel, then inside to warm up with drinks at Tavern on the Green.

She contemplated ordering a bourbon Manhattan in honor of her grandmother. "I was always allowed to 'steal' the Amarena cherry garnish when Bubbe wasn't looking," she shared, shedding her hoodie. Just thinking about it made her mouth water; she had always had a taste for both sweet *and* sour, and those cherries were the best of both worlds.

"Did your grandma give you that necklace?" he asked. "You play with it, when you bring her up," he added.

Nora hadn't realized it, but the tiny Chai symbol at her throat had become a chakra touchpoint. More so in recent days.

Chai meant life, which her grandmother had certainly been full of. Reminding Nora with that mantra to always be true to herself.

"She gave the best presents. This to wear as a Bat Mitzvah, on the bimah. She gifted the famous Jocko, too." Nora smiled, touching her necklace once more before reaching for the drinks menu. "But like your grandpa, her best gift was her advice."

When the waiter arrived, she decided to go for a more modern cocktail, one in spirit with the season. "A Fig & Pomegranate Martini, please."

Beck doubled the order, then leaned in. "That's a bit classier than those Peppermintinis Hedstrom was throwing back yesterday."

"Oy, that toothpaste in a glass? Gross."

"Not such a bad idea, toothpaste in a glass – especially after your bagels."

She laughed, and he grinned back.

Not one poppy seed to be found in his perfect teeth, dammit.

"Feels like longer ago than just yesterday, doesn't it?" Beck continued, his thumbs tracing concentric circles on the leather table top. "I feel like I've known you longer."

She watched, entranced. Remembering how he had made similar patterns on her skin last night. Wanting that again, despite her better judgement.

"I've been thinking...it feels easy," she said softly. "Like a Sunday morning kind of easy." She took a big sip of her Pom & Fig. *Ugh, that sounded so cringe.* If Avi were here, he would Lionel Ritchie all over that.

Sitting in the cozy confines of the tavern felt safe and familiar. And not just because it was a place of memories from the cherry-stealing days of Bubbe bringing her there for hot chocolates in tea cups. With its old-but-new worn parquet wood floors, green velvet and gilded mirrors.

With Beck.

He was the last person who should make her feel safe. But with his warm hands within reach, the woozy cocktails, and the afternoon sun studding everything golden, she felt that and more.

Safe. Familiar. Seen. Content.

"But I don't want it to be Sunday yet," she confessed. "Because Mondays come next. And Mondays are hard."

"Let's not rush anything." His dark eyes channeled many meanings as he glanced up at her. "This holiday is all about making things last, no?"

Alex had made Nora laugh with his toothpaste crack, which was even more rewarding than the tavern's heat and booze after their long winter walk.

But was there truth serum in his martini? Because now he wanted to grab her hands and tell her that if it were up to him, she would never have a difficult Monday again in her life.

Did he have the authority – or the right – to promise her that?

Unless Nora told him what was troubling her at work,

he didn't know how he could make that happen. Or if she would even let him.

Unless you fire her, Alex.

That would be one down, only twenty-six to go.

She'd pulled the tie out of her bun, allowing her hair to tumble over her shoulders. Bare shoulders, he noted. That thermal Henley she wore had looked practical and innocent, but once she'd taken off her zip-up hoodie...the unexpected glimpse of her pale skin from the open-shoulder design of her top nearly sent him over the edge.

The edge he had contemplated taking care of in the shower this morning, but not when she ended up ten feet away in her striped socks, drinking his hotel room Nespresso.

The shower had at least cleared his head. Up until now. As had the bracing air outdoors. Now, time had slowed down to the point where it felt like it could go either way. Backward or forward. Could they rewind to that connection prior to the lighting of the first candle? Or fast-forward to see what the second night would bring?

He decided he was content with the here and now, just getting to know Nora in this moment, for the –

"...Present! Just one," Nora clapped her hands, excited, bringing him back from outer space. "It'll be fun, right? To open something tonight after candles? I know just the place."

They took their time, making their way downtown. Nora was the best kind of tour guide – combining off-the-beaten-path surprises with must-see landmark spots, weaving stories in for context. If she had an agenda, she was certainly flexible when something caught either of their attention.

She hadn't been kidding when she said they'd be

outside for most of the day, but Alex hadn't minded one bit. It was fun to watch her play tourist in her own town. One minute she was a jaded New Yorker, the next; wide-eyed as a child, laughing with delight.

"What do you mean, you don't have Christmas tree vendors on the streets?" she asked, incredulous, when he admitted to never having seen a transplanted forest of cut and tied trees just hanging out on the sidewalk. "Where do people get their trees from?"

"Places called farms, Nora. Or nurseries? Pretty sure the entire rest of the country would agree with me." He laughed. The city street did smell pretty amazing, though. Between the sharp scent of fresh pine, and the fragrant roasting of candied nuts from vendors on just about every corner they'd passed. "If that blows your mind, imagine if I took you to see a corn maze."

He *could* imagine taking her to Des Moines. It had a historic East Village, not so unlike the one they were walking in now. There was a lot more to see in Iowa than just corn. And hayseeds.

They'd had a late lunch at Veselka, which served kasha varnishkes almost as good as he remembered Gran Leah's. Then espresso drinks served out of a funky Airstream trailer near Astor Place before hitting the Strand Bookstore, which had also been on Alex's list of places to see.

Nora bought a cookbook there for Talia. And a *Nice Jewish Guys* calendar for Sylvie. An annual tradition, Nora explained. "I keep hoping she'll get the hint and manifest a new poster boy for herself."

"Avi no good for her?"

Nora sighed. "You know that thing some people say about soulmates, how they're not necessarily the one you're meant to be with? And more like the person who challenges you, and pushes you out of your boundaries? Avi and Sylvie have been pushing and pulling at each other since Israel. I don't think it's the healthiest thing for either of them." She shrugged. "But who am I to judge?"

Alex was not one to talk, either. Sheila, his last girlfriend, had pretty much ended them when she moved to Chicago after grad school. There had been no soul, no challenge, and no pull to follow her there. Plus Grandpa My had started going downhill at that point, leaving Alex to believe that staying within the boundaries of Des Moines was where he needed to be.

"Here we are," Nora pointed. "This is Union Square Park. But this time of year, it turns into a holiday market."

"You're not kidding." Alex whistled under his breath. There had to be over a hundred red and white tents lining the various pathways of the park. If Nora could navigate this, she would have no problem in his dinky hometown corn maze.

She grabbed his hand to cross the street, which was more like three intersecting streets, and led them into the park. "We have a bunch of European-type Christmas markets back home, German and Dutch-inspired. But nothing like this."

It was a true holiday market, with New York's pot finally melting and blending its sights, sounds and smells. Alex noticed German *stollen* fruitcake and Glühwein and next to a French hot chocolate stall, empanadas sharing space with Moroccan kebabs, even sufganiyot and another type of puffy donuts being sold single or by the dozen.

"Those are *buñuelos* – Sephardic donuts for Hanukkah," Nora said. "So good with honey. Here, try."

She insisted on buying one, since he had picked up the check for drinks and lunch. And holding it while he took a bite, getting honey all over both of them in the process. Alex didn't mind – it was a far cry from the lox and whitefish she had tried to repel him with earlier, but he didn't dare point that out.

Corrugated metal roofs, some trimmed with lights, others with green boughs, shielded vendors and shoppers alike from the elements, but they were very much outdoors as they decided where to start their Hanukkah shopping.

"Okay, I know how you love your rules, so... twenty minutes?" he suggested. "And under twenty dollars?"

"You're on, Beckman. I'll meet you under that subway sign there."

"It's a date, Ruben."

Nora couldn't keep the grin off her face as she floated dreamily from stall to stall. Fingering silks and wools, trying to dream up a perfect gift for Beck.

It's a date, Ruben.

All right, she knew it was just a figure of speech. And this day had been all about low-pressure, totally platonic hospitality. But she hadn't had a date in forever, beyond a few failed app attempts, always at coffee shops that usually ended as awkwardly as they started. Oh, and her and Talia's last attempt to mutually matchmake for each other, to which they had both vowed *never again.* Funny how two best friends could have such utterly different ideas when it came to men in this city.

Nora remembered she had yet to respond to Talia's earlier text. She quickly took a moment to shoot her friend two photos back – Beck in profile as he contemplated the Central Park menorah, and her fancy Fig & Pom martini sitting on its Tavern on the Green cocktail napkin – with little context:

It's after noon, but that's all I know...

She made a mental note to call Talia later. Right now, she was on the clock.

Still, it was easy to spend a few of her twenty minutes picking up some items for them to nosh on after they lit the candles. Libby was the better fridge-stocker of the two, and with Talia not far, meal planning rarely fell upon Nora's shoulders. But part of being a good tour guide was sharing your favorite parts of the city and that meant its food, too.

How about being a good Jewish wife?

Oh God, had her mother just taken the N train to 14th Street – from Florida – just to nag her? Ruth Ruben's voice sounded clear as a bell in Nora's head. So clear, Nora felt the need to glance over each shoulder (and possibly spit three times to ward off evil, but she refrained) just to make sure her snowbird mother hadn't flapped her way back up north.

And there – she saw it.

What no good Jewish wife would ever buy a man if she wanted him for a husband.

It was glorious, it was perfect, and it was $19.95.

Chapter Eleven

"Close your eyes, hold out your hands."

Nora's eyes sparkled in the light of the three candles dwindling down. They'd recited the prayers, without a boatful of other people to carry them, and Alex enjoyed the way their voices had twined together.

Her menorah, a modern one with its *shamash* sitting slightly higher on one side rather than in the middle, had served as their centerpiece, lighting up Nora's coffee table as they sat on floor pillows to eat. Briny olives, hummus and pita, and cubed cheese made the perfect finger foods to snack on, and an antidote to all the fried delicacies they had enjoyed the night before. Alex had bought a hard cider from an upstate vendor at the holiday market, and its hints of ginger and cinnamon with the apple brought a bit of sweetness to the meal.

He did as he was told, and was rewarded with a bulky lump rolled in tissue paper. They hadn't bothered with holiday wrapping, having arrived at Nora's apartment famished, and just in time to light the candles.

Alex slid his finger under a small length of tape that kept his present rolled, and the tissue fell away. "Oh…wow."

It was pretty much the tackiest Hanukkah sweater he had ever seen. And his sister owned a rainbow-tasseled one that proclaimed *We Be Flaming*, so that was saying a lot.

Nora's selection was blue knit with white lettering that read *"TOO LIT TO QUIT"* and boasted a big yellow menorah in the center. A border of dancing dreidels ringed the neck, the cuffs and the bottom of the sweater.

"You said you could ugly sweater with the best of them," Nora howled with laughter as Alex gamely shed his flannel shirt and pulled off his T-shirt to model his gift. "Wait, wait, here's the best part."

She practically climbed into his lap, fiddling with the hem. "There we go." The monstrosity actually had a battery-powered *switch*, and suddenly he was blinking; all eight candles, in unison.

"Oh, you're going to pay for this," he warned, laughing and pushing up his sleeves.

"Oh, I already did." she mocked. "19.95, including tax."

"I love it. Honestly. I'm going to wear it to the office on Monday."

"Not if I steal it from you and wear it first."

She sat back on her heels, biting her lip in anticipation as Alex leaned to grab her gift from his coat.

It was a smallish box, but he hoped it contained a big pay-off. He'd found it about half-way through his twenty-minute search for just the right present. After all, her grandmother's gifts were a hard act to follow. But this…he thought she would appreciate this.

"Happy Hanukkah, Ruben."

She shook it, smiling at him. Then quirked a brow when it made no sound whatsoever. It felt light enough to be empty. But Alex had watched the vendor pack and seal the box himself. "Go on...open it. It won't bite."

As she worked to unclasp the box, Alex had momentary second thoughts. That this was too personal. Or she would take it the wrong way. Her gift had been all in fun, while this...

A red pompom fell out of the box as she tilted it, then yarn. A glassine envelope containing two black buttons. Followed by a tiny sewing kit and a bag of cotton batting. And last, Nora pulled out the pièce de résistance: a pair of brown and white knit socks.

"Original Rockford Red Heel?" she practically whispered, as if it were too good to be true. "Oh, Alex."

It was the first time she had used his given name. It did things to him that he couldn't put a label or a price tag on.

"I know there's no replacing Jocko. Or your grandma's gift. It didn't feel right to just buy you a ready-made one..."

The whole stall had been filled with the finished products –sock monkeys in different colors, sizes, genders. But when he'd spied the option for a Do-It-Yourself Sock Monkey Kit, he instantly knew.

Her eyes filled. "This is...this is amazing. And the most thoughtful – thank you." Her voice caught. She hugged the socks close to her chest. Then, thinking better of it, she pulled off her striped socks and pushed her feet into the new ones. "Breaking them in first." She laughed, stretching out her legs to admire her feet, and wiggling her toes.

"Oh wait. There's more."

"I hope you didn't go over budget," she warned.

He dug deep into his jeans pocket, coming out with the errant jingle bell he'd saved from his suit pocket. "I think his hat could use this."

Alex Beckman, son of Alice and Sam, grandson of Leah and Hal, had fallen asleep on Nora's couch.

The late night and subsequent long day had caught up with both of them. Nora felt a wave of exhaustion carrying their dishes to the sink, just as her phone lit up with a text from Avi.

> Jay scored 9:30 rez @ Enclave, say you'll come. Bring Brioni!

Nine-thirty wasn't a.m. and Enclave wasn't Sunday brunch. It was a late night Russian supper club in Brooklyn, complete with over-the-top dancers, endless blini, pelmeni and black caviar, flowing vodka and live music. There was no way Jay had reserved a table for less than twenty people, and it was always a built-in party...or more like crashing a wedding where you knew no one but still had a blast.

In other words, perfect for the final stop on her and Beck's tour.

If only they had time for a nap...

"Beck, I'm thinking – "

She returned to the living room to find him on his side, long legs hanging off the end of the sectional, arms crossed in that hideous sweater. At least he had powered it down first. Face relaxed, lashes perfectly fanned on his cheeks.

I'm thinking that looks really comfortable.

There was just enough room to slide onto the cushions in front of him. *Just a disco nap.*

His arms instinctively enveloped her, pulling her deeper onto the plush upholstery. Into his warmth. Like perfect spoons in a drawer.

Just twenty minutes. Tucking her head under his chin, she let her eyes close. *That's all we need*.

"Norrr..."

A vibration against her neck tickled her awake.

"Nora...what are we doing?"

"We're going...to...Brighton Beach." Her lips could barely pull the words out, she was so comfortable. And her apartment building was so quiet. Way past nine-thirty p.m. quiet.

"Any place...with a beach...sounds far from here." Alex mumbled against her neck, making her giggle.

They had upset the cutlery drawer symmetry in their sleep. No longer resting spoons. She'd flipped, he'd shifted. His mouth on her neck, her hand cupping his very muscular butt.

"There's a nightclub there...with fire dancers."

"Fire ants."

"No, *dancers*. Or maybe it's...fire eaters? Can't...recall." Her spoon was very, very content. Not upset in the least.

"No...fire ants...eating my skin!"

Beck pulled himself upright, clawing at the Hanukkah sweater.

Nora, more alert now, jumped up to help him pull it off. Sure enough, even in the dim light from the bare window, evidence of a rash was spreading, red and angry-looking, across his chest, stomach and down his arms.

"Oh my God, I set a plague upon you with a cheap street vendor sweater!" she wailed. "Hold on, I have Benadryl...oh, and aloe! I have an aloe plant in my room, hang on." She rushed down the hall, sliding in her new socks and flipping every light switch along the way.

Even though Libby teased Nora about her black thumb,

she had somehow kept an aloe plant alive since college. Now, she knew it was for a reason. She broke off a thick, juicy leaf to get at its gel.

"Nora, I'm going to be fine." Beck had followed her, and was now standing shirtless in her bedroom doorway. "Really, it's all good."

"No, it's not! It's all my fault!" She slid her hands, slick with aloe, over his hot-to-the-touch shoulders. "I'll make a terrible Jewish wife!"

"What?" he laughed, stilling her hands once they reached his chest. "Look. It's already going away. Now that the air's hit it. I'm fine."

He was. Smooth, solid pecs. Cut, muscular stomach. The rash had all but disappeared. *So fine.* When she realized she was admiring the thin dusting of dark hair that disappeared into the button of his jeans, she jerked her head up. *Oh gosh.* Bedhead again.

Now his hands were sticky from touching hers. But she didn't mind one bit as he traced his fingertips around the hems of her cold shoulder top, where the cut-out pattern exposed her skin. "Been wanting to do that," he breathed. Cider and cinnamon still lingered as she tilted her head to softly meet his lips where they fell on hers in a velvet crush.

She pulled him with her, knowing the bed would catch them. Their mouths more eager now, hands exploring. She yanked at her own top, yearning to feel his bare skin hot against hers. Beck sat back only long enough to assist her, then was all over her again, mouth on her lacy bra strap, across her cleavage, fingers deftly popping the clasp at her spine. She sighed as he pulled her bra from between them, leaving nothing between the press of their bodies.

"Not your fault at all." He let out a shaky breath as she worked to undo his button fly where his hard ridge strained against it. "The sweater either." He grinned. "I should've left my T-shirt on...as a barrier."

"Speaking of..." Nora remembered between kisses, shucking his jeans as gracefully as she could. "...I've got a few in my purse, courtesy of Jonah Klein."

"Such a mensch, that guy."

She reached back toward her nightstand where she had left her clutch bag, but Beck took full advantage; sliding down the stretch of her body, peeling off her leggings. Next, her new socks, one by one. "No need for future Jocko to bear witness." Then, drugging her with kisses along her inner thigh as he worked his way back up.

"And no rush," he whispered, his mouth hot and tantalizingly close to her most sensitive spot. She sucked a breath of air as his tongue touched down. "I'm all for making it last."

Even Alex's imagination – and his dirty mind – couldn't hold a candle to what reality had dropped in his lap. Literally. Nora, all of her. Mewing, sighing, quivering Nora beautifully above him. That first wave of attraction upon first sight of her had Tsunamied as he had spent more time with her, gotten to know her. Tonight, being able to touch her, taste her...feel her break against him. It had been her name on his lips as he lost himself in her.

He'd always taken his time with other girlfriends. Hell, he and Sheila took six months to finally get around to it. Lights off, covers up, that's-the-way-she-wanted-things Sheila. It was different with Nora. And not just because she had set every bulb ablaze in her tiny apartment during her first-aid quest and they hadn't bothered to shut them off.

Although to watch her...damn, he was getting turned on again.

Nora was different, period. Time had done that slow-down trick again, as he held her in his arms, tracing circles on her fully bare shoulder. Waiting for his heart, at least, to return to its normally scheduled programming. He didn't think his life was capable of it.

"So what was that comment, earlier? Something about a Jewish wife?"

Her mussed hair rubbed against his cheek as she moved to cover her face, groaning a laugh.

"I just had this...oh, it's stupid. I let my mother get in my head about something. Don't worry, it didn't follow us into bed." She knocked on the wooden headboard for good measure. "*Kina hora*."

She looked even more glamorous, sitting up and looking at him with the sheet crumpled against her boobs and a long bare leg bent between his own, than in that dress — on that boat. The color in her cheeks, dark eyes alight. But she didn't say anything further on the subject.

"I like you like this." She ran her fingers through where his hair now curled at the ends, rumpling it. "The all-sexed-up with no sleep look."

"All you."

"Hmm, the aloe may've helped."

She happily stretched up against him as he laughed.

"Did I tell you about the time my mom almost killed my dad with a deli sandwich?"

Nora gasped, shaking her head against his chest.

"She wasn't even a Jewish wife yet. They were dating, and he was working endlessly on his Ph.D. dissertation. She'd promised to bring him lunch, but...you know, she's an artist. She got deep into a project, lost track of time. So he calls her, he's starving. She runs out, stopping at the deli near the campus, forgets to bring money..."

"Artists," Nora tsked.

"When she explained her plight the owner said no problem, that my dad was a good customer. And did she want his usual. Which she gratefully accepted."

"But let me guess. He had no usual?"

"Nope. And not only that, but it was some sort of ham salad sandwich, which she just figured was tuna. My dad had never tasted ham in his life." Alex chuckled at the thought, having heard the story a hundred times but never having told it. Nora gripped his arm now, invested.

He wanted to spend the foreseeable future with her hair against his bare chest, telling her stories. Having her react in all the right ways.

"But that wasn't what did it. It was the bread, some sort of multigrain. With sesames. And she didn't know he was highly allergic."

"Oh my God. That's horrible." She buried her face in his neck.

"Luckily, she got him to Drake's student health center and they gave him epinephrine right away. It all worked out, obviously. Or I wouldn't be here. So, happily ever after and all that."

"Not if he can't eat halvah!"

Alex laughed. "Ham, but no halvah." He played with her hair, twirling it absently. A moment went by. Then another. She sighed against him, relaxing.

"I think sometimes," he began, stifling a yawn, "it's impossible to really know what's best for someone – or even for yourself. Sometimes you just have to approach it together and figure it out...the hard way. But if the good intention is there..."

"If you're trying to make me feel better about the sweater," she whispered, "It's totally working."

If it was possible to laugh in your sleep – he was. Falling deep into it with his arms full of Nora and all the lights on.

Chapter Twelve

Nora woke up with two regrets: she had no cream for coffee in the apartment, and she still hadn't told Beck about what was going on at Britesmith.

Well, she could remedy one thing immediately, at least.

"Beck..."

Would you believe me if I told you –

He didn't stir at the whisper of his name, or the kiss on his shoulder.

You're not going to like this, but –

She studied him in sleep. His fingers curled possessively around her pillow. Lips pursed, heavy brow relaxed.

Okay, maybe coffee first. Talk later.

The corner bodega was used to seeing her roll in at all hours for all things – in pajama bottoms and UGGs at three p.m. when she was in need of a can of chicken soup and tampons. After clubbing at one a.m. with her girls for Gatorade and string cheese. Today, she was a normal person buying normal things at a normal hour. Grabbing Half-and-Half, bagels, *The New York Times*. In Beck's Drake University T-shirt and braless because she had no idea where he threw it last night, mind you; plus yesterday's leggings, which could be considered walk-of-shame attire. Nonetheless, it felt right for a Sunday morning.

Easy.

She loved walking through her quiet neighborhood, the empty streets at this hour. It was the time of day where she felt like she had Manhattan all to herself, and Manhattan had her back. She returned to find coffee on, and a shirtless man at her stove. Barefoot, and in just his jeans.

I could get used to this.

"So that's where my shirt went." He pointed a spatula at her. "How do you like your eggs?"

"Over hard." She shed her jacket. "How do you like your sugar?"

He leaned over his shoulder for a kiss. "With coffee and cream."

"Cute *and* has Beastie Boys knowledge?" She reached into the cupboard for mugs. "I really underestimated Iowa."

"Yeah ya did." He grabbed her around the waist, one-handed, still wielding the spatula. "Mmm, hot city girl in my T-shirt with nothing underneath? I don't think I ordered that with my coffee."

She twined her arms around his neck. "So send me back."

He gazed down at her, biting back his smile. "Never... unless it's back to bed. And I bring you breakfast there."

"I have rules."

"Of course you do."

"Pants off. Because no subway clothes on my sheets."

They made a cozy nest – pillows propped, coffee within reach. Nora lost the leggings again but kept the T on, since he liked it so much. Beck followed suit, kicking his jeans off and serving her eggs and bagels in his boxers. They traded sections of the Sunday *Times* – allowed in bed because technically it was reading material – and stories about their favorite snow days as kids. Because, as if the universe had decided things weren't cozy enough, snow had begun to fall.

"I wish..." Nora began. *So many things in this moment.* It was hard to even put into words, but she couldn't remember the last time she felt so settled. In the moment. Not stuck in her head.

"You can tell me," Beck set aside the paper, reached for her. "Anything, Nora. Seriously."

She climbed into his lap, hands meeting his and entwining fingers. He tilted his head up, watching her. "A part of me wishes it would keep snowing all day, so hard that the office couldn't open tomorrow and your flight would be cancelled Tuesday and we could just stay here, like this."

It came out in a rush – she knew she was babbling, but it was hard to contain it once it started. "But another part of me knows..."

He kissed her as her voice broke. Leaned up to kiss her eyelids so no tears would come. "Nora...do you trust me?"

Nora opened her eyes, nodding. Lightly touching her forehead to his.

"It's a two-way street, you know."

"Unlike Sixth Avenue," she muttered. When Alex raised a brow in question, she added, "When I couldn't go after you the other night. In the Town Car, because my heels were too high and the driver – never mind. You were saying?"

"I'm saying, I trust you, too."

He locked eyes with her, and she felt all at once the vulnerability and intensity of what they had shared wordlessly last night. That vivid, tender whirlwind, right before they came together. Opening parts of themselves for the other. To each other. There had been trust there too.

From the moment she had reached for his hand in the crowd while leaving the party, there had been trust.

Leap...and the net will appear.

"Hedstrom has been stealing from Britesmith employees. For years. And I think I'm to blame."

Alex was hearing Nora speak the words, but they weren't fully sinking in. Something about 401(k)s and missing contributions. Audits and trustees. She was leaning so softly against him, her breasts heavy under the thin cotton of his shirt. He closed his eyes and breathed her in, wanting to memorize her scent, this intimacy. To shut out all the reality of what she was admitting to him.

Grandpa My had been so careful.

There *had* been audits. Forensic accountants. Due diligence to make sure everything was on the up and up with the target company pre-close, because it was a hell of a lot easier than trying to untangle themselves, post-close. Britesmith was not Myers and Sons' first rodeo when it came to mergers and acquisitions. They knew what flags to look for in a company's financial records.

But the plan assets Nora was talking about were not considered company assets. Employee contributions – whether they were deposited properly or not – would not show up on any balance sheet, positive or negative.

"He was just 'borrowing' it." She dropped his hands so she could hang air quotes around her words. "He called it 'unclothing Peter to clothe Paul,' whatever that means."

"I think that's a saint thing." Although he was pretty sure he'd learned in business school it was a Ponzi scheme thing.

Not that Hedstrom was capable of reaching Bernie Madoff proportions – he was just a small-change businessman who'd made a series of foolish decisions. Keeping Britesmith afloat just long enough for a larger company like Myers to swoop in was probably more dumb luck on his part, coupled with loyal employees – like Nora – playing kingmaker.

Whether unwittingly or...not so much.

"I thought you were HR. Not accounting – how would you know?"

"I am...well, I'm People Operations. That's what we call it. He made me People Operations Officer."

Nora's job title was POO? It was no wonder she felt so shitty about Britesmith.

"I convinced people I hired – good, hardworking people – to contribute. Believing Hedstrom when he said he'd handle the investment portion of it. Not knowing he was basically using their funds like a ninety-day checking account," she gulped. "And I only found out because...these are my *people*, Beck. And one of them came to me. For help."

She rose shakily to her knees, shifting her balance to move off of him. He stilled her, hands stroking up her thighs. "It's not your fault. Any misappropriation or falsification on his part..."

Was now his family's company's problem.

"How much are we talking about? And why didn't you report it?"

She batted his hands away. "Does it really matter how much at the end of the day? What's a drop in the bucket to companies like yours could be someone else's entire nest egg."

This time, she did spring up, catapulting herself off the bed. She hastily piled plates, gathered their mugs. "Try two dozen nest eggs! And I did report it. I went right to the top: your grandfather. He never replied."

She left him sitting stunned in the middle of her bed. Trying to process.

Take care of Britesmith.

As if those words hadn't been cryptic enough, now everything felt tinged with a double meaning. Had his grandfather known? His uncle?

"It doesn't matter anymore. Problem apparently solved. Even if our year-end bonuses helped take the brunt of it."

Cut twenty-seven by year-end.

Just a number.

Now it was Alex's turn to feel like crap. For what he was about to say.

"It does still matter. I'm pretty sure it's the reason I'm here, Nora."

Chapter Thirteen

Bulletproof Nora was back, standing in the doorway. His flannel in her hand. *Okay then.* If she was going to send him on his way, he may as well lay all the cards on the table. She would know exactly what to expect, as People Operations Officer, come tomorrow morning.

"I was sent to reduce your staff by half."

"By Hedstrom?"

"No. He doesn't know." He approached her. "That I know of. Unless he and my uncle...it doesn't matter, because I'm not planning to do it. Not their way, anyway."

Nora gave him a long stare. Then tossed him his flannel. "Then I know exactly where we are going today."

"Another custom New Yorker tour for the Hayseed?"

"Something like that."

She turned on her heel and marched toward the bathroom, discarding his T-shirt along the way and leaving him with the glorious view of her panties-clad ass before the door slammed shut and the shower hissed on.

He took it he was not invited.

Scrubbing a hand over his mouth, he collected his clothes and got dressed. Tried not to think of her naked and twenty-feet away. Did the dishes. Tried not to think of the penalties for IRS fraud.

Use your head. For once, he didn't give Uncle Marty's words the mental middle finger. He would look at all the facts before jumping to any conclusions. There was nothing he could do until Monday morning – the day he was supposed to arrive at Britesmith in the first place.

Nora rubbed steam off the mirror and contemplated herself, post-leap. She had followed Eli's advice, and wasn't sure where it had gotten her. But one thing she knew for a fact: hiding out in bed with Alex Beckman was not a viable solution for the day. Not after the bomb he just dropped.

Was it coincidence that Beck had been sent to chop heads? And roughly the same number as those impacted by Hedstrom's dirty little secret?

She laid out a clean towel and found a spare toothbrush. Hospitality was never far from her mind, in all its shapes and forms. "All yours," she called, and went to get dressed.

They hit 46th Street. Nora made a point of detouring into Times Square, just enough for Beck to realize that the heart of Broadway beat straight through to the veins of its narrower surrounding streets. And even if you didn't recognize the names on all the marquees, they were lit just as bright...even on a Sunday afternoon.

Matinee day.

Britesmith may not have had the biggest or the most Broadway theater accounts of its concessions competitors, but the roster it maintained was reputable. And Nora was proud to have had a hand in staffing them – from the art deco lobby bar of an intimate six—hundred-seat gem to an opulent venue's coat-check responsible for the belongings of its fifteen-hundred theatergoers.

She knew the people who closed the curtains after a standing ovation, and she knew the people who opened the doors for the day. If you weren't part of a union, you were part of a contract like the ones Britesmith held. But working show after show, you became part of the same family.

It was, as she had mentioned to Beck that first night, the thing she loved most about working in the theaters.

"Are you sure we're supposed to be in here?" Beck asked, as they entered the lobby of the first theater. "Or let me guess – another VIP perk?"

She smirked and allowed him to open a second set of heavy doors.

Workers were humming along with quiet efficiency. Bar staff re-stocking, a cashier counting bills in front of her register at the merch stall. Two identically-dressed ushers carrying a velvet rope and its poles toward the restrooms.

"Quiet, right? It's the calm before the storm."

They approached a glass counter holding not just the usual brands of wrapped candy and bagged chips, but also snacks unique to the show. *Yes,* she silently cheered. Tia London was working today.

"You got any Swedish Fish back there?" Nora taunted to get her attention.

"Nora! You coming to bail me out?" The tall girl reached her slim arms across the glass counter to embrace her.

"Hey Tia, nah – busman's holiday. This is my friend, Beck. Beck... Tia London."

"Oh, it's officially London-Lang now." She grinned, shaking Beck's hand. "Hi, Beck."

"I'm so glad everything worked out," Nora started, which was all Tia needed to launch into her story.

"Shoot, without your help, I would've lost every deposit! All those wedding vendors needing payment." She shook her natural springy curls and turned to Beck. "My girl here worked some miracles after I tried to dip into my 401(k) to borrow ten large and came up short. Something was all messed up with my balance, I don't know what, but she got me squared away quick."

"Every penny," Nora confirmed, glancing at Beck pointedly. "And I'm working on getting software approved for the budget so you will be able to check on your account activity yourself, at any time."

"I know borrowing against it wasn't the best way, since I gotta pay interest now. But weddings in New York are crazy – I was just glad I'd been saving for so long. We got a lot of gifts, though, so I'll be paying myself back real soon," she laughed.

A roar of applause and chatter swept up the aisles and into the large space, as ushers propped open doors.

"Here we go! Nice meeting you. Here, guys – it's on me."

Tia tossed Beck a bag of Swedish Fish and turned her attention to the well-dressed customers flooding the lobby for intermission.

"Quick," Nora grabbed Beck's hand, "the bar gets mobbed fast." They hit the one on the mezzanine before the thirsty balcony folks made it down the steps.

"Hi, Angelo. Two of your bestsellers, please!"

The old man behind the bar had a yellow-toothed smile that lit up at Nora's request. He shuffled a bit but was deft in returning with two snifter-type glasses. "It's called 'Drink Your Feelings,' after the opening number."

He waved away Beck's offer of bills, so Beck stuffed the tip jar silly instead.

"Angelo's been designing drinks to go with shows since...since when?"

"Young lady, you know my age from my personnel file so I will say no more." He began to pour champagne for two older women in their minks.

"Wow, what is in this?" Beck marveled at the burnt orange concoction.

Without missing a beat, Angelo began to recite a laundry list of ingredients, as he made change, opened beer bottles and swiped credit cards.

"You got your bourbon, your cherry liqueur, then you add a drizzle from the honey bear. No more than three dashes of chocolate bitters. A swizzle spoon of orange marmalade and – don't you dare." He took the gummy fish Nora was about to add to her drink right from her hand and laid it on his tongue like a communion wafer.

She laughed. "Not trying to improve on perfection, Angelo. You hear from Bennett lately?"

"Wonder Boy is working in their HQ now. They just landed that big new Disney musical."

"Hot damn, tell him congrats next time you see him. Truly our loss."

Nora toasted him with her glass and they maneuvered to a velvet bench on the landing of the stairs so they could sip their drinks and people-watch.

"So Hedstrom wanted to fire Angelo for not sticking to a classic drinks menu. A bunch of us went to bat for him – Parker even did polling on his days off and created a spread-sheet to prove the custom drinks' popularity and profit margin." She took a long sip. "Damn, I could drink my feelings every day. Even without a Swedish Fish garnish."

"These are all Britesmithers?" Beck asked.

Nora counted with a pointer finger. "Only five in Front of House. But this is one of the smaller theaters we work with. We had six."

"Was that Bennett you mentioned?"

"Yeah. When his wife had their second baby, he came up with a brilliant idea for plastic cups with sippy lids on them, for theater-goers to be able to return safely to their seats with their drinks. Hedstrom nixed it, saying it would be 'controversial.' I don't blame Bennett, but he moved to one of our competitors, who rolled out that idea faster than you can say 'paternity leave.' Which, by the way, they gave him, too."

They shared the bag of gummies and watched as the Britesmith employees took on the crowds with a friendly greeting and quick service. "It's different than the ballparks in many ways, obviously. But in other ways, exactly the same."

Angelo was pointing at a young couple nervously waiting at the back of his line, assuring them he'd get to them before the bell chimed.

"During hiring, I look for people with hospitality experience, sure. But if they understand theater, it's a plus."

"A-plus, Ruben." Beck's praise burned bright and warm like the bourbon, all the way to their next stop.

"This matinee started an hour later than the last one, so..." Nora flashed her ID at the box office worker of a much bigger operation right on 42nd Street.

In they swept, but whatever performance was happening didn't seem to be contained to the stage. You could hear heavy rock music thumping from behind the closed doors. The lobby itself was much dimmer – still quite cavernous and grand but was going for a wholly different aesthetic.

Alex recognized the girl pinning a black T-shirt emblazoned with the show logo to the wall of the merch stall – although combat boots and piercings could've been the required uniform.

"You came! Finally!" April jumped down from her stepladder and hugged Nora before giving a shy wave to Alex. She pointed out elements with a black-lacquered nail, including a replica of an iron maiden that people could step into for photos, and a bar that was frothing with dry ice and neon green "shots" in clear plastic syringes.

This is still Broadway? Alex thought Des Moines had arrived when they finally got the touring production of *Hamilton*. This was next level...and probably wouldn't make it to the Midwest for three to five more years. They followed April down a side walkway toward the stage, where strobe lights could be seen stuttering from the gap in the aisle's curtain.

"It's almost intermission!" Even hollering, April's voice was lost to the crescendo. A small group of people huddled in the wings, dressed similarly to the playbill photos hanging outside and heavily made-up. They held trays strapped to their neck like old-time cigarette girls, but everything else about them screamed BDSM steampunk.

Alex caught Nora's attention and gestured. "Are those actors from the performance?"

"They're waitstaff." She leaned close, her murmur laced with liqueur and a hint of Swedish Fish. "It's an immersive performance, so when the actors leave the stage, this concession crew takes over and fits in seamlessly."

"Nora came up with their costumes!" April praised. Alex turned to see if Nora had anything to say for herself, but she was sucking on one of the green syringes plucked from a staffer's tray and shrugging modestly.

The house lights didn't exactly go up, but the theater went from pitch black to red light district. The staff sashayed out and began slinging drinks and hand-helds to the crowd, who raised credit cards high and snapped pictures. Alex estimated about half stayed in the theater, while the rest of the audience moved up the aisles for their twenty-minute reality check and pee break.

Nora squeezed his hand and gestured with her chin. "Young love."

April had her arms wrapped around a stick figure of a guy coming toward them, smelling of clean sweat and greasepaint. He looked more like a graverobbing rock star than a trained tenor, but Alex recognized him as the lead from the poster. He tipped his top hat to them, and they continued up the aisle.

"April's boyfriend, Tommy. She was my first Britesmith hire – graphic design is her side hustle, but her true love is this." She swept her hands around, before dropping her voice. "She's young and entirely too trusting, but smart. Went right for the max contribution and company match. But hasn't been with Britesmith long enough to be vested."

In other words, a perfect candidate for Hedstrom's nefarious fuckery.

The waitstaff hustled by with empty trays, probably wanting to get one last refill in before intermission was over. A couple of them fist-bumped Nora as they passed.

"Even without makeup, you wouldn't have recognized

them from the holiday party. So many of our hires do have acting jobs off-Broadway, in addition to their day job. Most of the people there were the corporate drones, like me."

"Hardly," Alex chastised. "I see eight-year-old you in those eyes, lighting up like they must've during the opening chant of *Lion King*." He took one of her hands, and inspected her fingers. She was luminous, even with the red glow of the lights casting eerie shadows on her pale skin. "And I see the straight-A costume major through college, designing those get-ups...which are fabulous, by the way. Future Jocko will be in good hands."

"Maybe I'll sew him a bondage costume, too," she laughed. Whatever had been in that shot loosened her up. Although perhaps it was just being around her people, Alex mused. In addition to the five from the first theater, there had to be double that here.

The house lights flashed, and a gong signaled a warning that intermission was wrapping up. "Oh my gosh, we have to get downtown!"

Nora and Alex swam upstream against the current of audience members excited for the final act. It was almost disconcerting when they finally burst through the exit door and onto the city street. The dreary afternoon was almost too bright compared to inside, and the bracing fresh air a sharp contrast to the close, humid heat of the theater. The snow they'd witnessed earlier had stopped, but clung fresh to the trees and dusted building awnings.

"Oh wow, it's still holiday time out here," Alex joked, as they were bombarded with Christmas songs pouring out of open shop doors, colored lights bedazzling food carts, and shoppers bumping their knees with their bags.

Hands in coat pockets, they raced into the closest

subway and Nora navigated them down to the West Village. "Last stop on our tour, I promise."

"Am I like some Jewish Ebenezer Scrooge, and you're the ghosts of Hanukkahs Past, Present, and Future?"

Nora really laughed now, unabashed. Like that first time making her crack up at the party, the throaty chuckle at the end just gut-punched him. He didn't know where they stood, or where they would find themselves, come Monday on the floors of Britesmith.

But it was the third night of Hanukkah and time with Nora felt as precious – no, precarious, as a certain cruse of oil. How long would it last?

Chapter Fourteen

"I should warn you... there's Off-Broadway and then there's Off-Off-Broadway." Nora held open the door of the Feldman Theater. It was Jewish Repertory, but you never knew what you might get.

Tonight it didn't really matter though. Because the show didn't start until six. But the seventy-seat theater had a holiday tradition that its actors loved to uphold.

"What the..." Beck looked back at the door, and forward again. Two steps down and they were transported into a 1940s Brooklyn brownstone. No separation from the stage and the audience; if you were sitting in the first row, you were essentially on the set. "So *this* is the ghost of Hanukkahs past."

Nora recognized some of the people on stage. They were setting an elaborate table. Linens, doilies, china, and an unassuming brass menorah. An older woman in a plain dress and apron bustled up to Beck. "You're looking thin, boychik! Come, have some *polkes* and *kishka* by the fire."

Nora suppressed a laugh. Beck's face clearly said he had

never tried *kishka* in his life, but had resigned himself to being polite and let himself be led away.

"Such a *shayna punim.*" A kindly-looking older man, his *yarmulke* sitting atop what remaining frizzled hair he had left, smiled and cupped Nora's chin. She had never known her grandfathers on either side of her family, but liked to think this was the dotage she would've received.

"Zeyde, Zeyde, can you teach us?" Two little kids, a boy and girl also in period clothing, ran across the "room" to the table, clutching dreidels in their hands. The boy hugged Nora's legs for good measure.

"Ask your parents, I need to ready the candles. It's almost sundown."

The little girl grinned up at Nora and took her hand, leading her to where Beck sat, by an electric fireplace, at an upright piano.

"I'll show you, sweetheart – while your...*father* plays us the song." She side-spoke to Beck, "Assuming you know The Dreidel Song?"

Beck smiled, clearly more comfortable now that he understood he was only playing a part. And that the kishksas were props. He started a dwindling, playful melody that began to romp around, not unlike a top might spin. The kids dropped to the floor and began to play, with Nora kneeling and pointing out the Hebrew letters.

More "family" joined them on the small stage – you could tell the audience apart from the actors, not just by their modern street clothes but by the wonderous looks on their faces. A young woman in a kerchief sat next to Beck at the piano and began to sing the lyrics to the traditional holiday song in a strong clear voice, encouraging the others to join in. Pretty much everyone knew it, whether Jewish or not.

Beck got an ovation, and the "Bubbe" figure rested her hands proudly on his shoulders after. "That's my boychik." She took Nora's hand first to help her to standing, then to place it in Beck's. "The *shadchan* made such a perfect match. We couldn't be happier for you – or more blessed."

Nora felt so in the moment, she almost opened her mouth to protest they had just met, and were just –

"*Bashert.*" Zeyde was back. The Yiddish concept meant different things to different people. *Meant to be.* The closest thing to soul mates, but she still wasn't sure she believed.

He gave Nora a wink before he gathered everyone, and there had to now be twenty people crowding around the dining room table. Teens, kids, adults, and some real grandparents as well. His "wife" handed him matches from her pocket, as if they had done this song-and-dance together for years now.

"*Baruch atah Adonai...*" Their spoken chorus wasn't as loud as their singing one, but those who knew led the group, Nora and Beck included. Slips of paper with the Hebrew written in phonetic English were passed around, and by the end everyone was in unison. "*...ner shel Hanukkah.*" All eyes on the *shamash* and its three candles in the antique menorah, all four flames dancing on the dimly lit stage.

Nora's fingers found Beck's hand down by the embroidered tablecloth. She ran her thumb into the center of his palm, and heard him draw a deep breath.

Everyone was clapping around them, but Nora and Beck didn't take back their hands. "Thank you all for coming to the Feldman Theater. Our shows this season – " Zeyde had dropped his old world accent to reveal his true Brooklynese and proceeded with his spiel.

"They call it their 'potluck' – it's a mix of an open house and an improv performance every year before their Sunday performances in December," Nora explained, as they made their way off the stage.

Many of the participants were now taking their seats in the audience, as others were just arriving, and the actors were heading backstage. "Looks like it's going to be a full house tonight."

"You want to stick around, visit with your staff?" Beck asked.

"Oh, there are no Britesmithers here. I just thought it would be something fun to do for the third night of Hanukkah." Nora waved a hand, laughing. "Totally worth it to see your reaction."

"Oh, you mean my *polke* face?" Beck gave her a playful shove as they made their way to the exit. "I played right along."

"You're a good sport," Nora said, pulling him close by the sides of his coat. Before she could talk herself out of it, she kissed him, right in the front vestibule.

"*Ope,* sorry – I don't see any mistletoe up there," he murmured, eyes upturned before focusing warmly on her. "Just a mezuzah."

"Any port in a storm, right?" she said softly, as he cupped her cheeks. "Look, I'm sorry I snapped at you earlier. Back at my place. It was just...when you assumed I didn't report – it was like you didn't believe me."

"I shouldn't have jumped to conclusions. I can see now you've had to shoulder so much alone. And seriously, how much you genuinely care for your staff. But well...then my shields went up, too. At the mention of my grandfather. It wasn't like him to leave anyone hanging like that."

Latecomers were pushing past them; it was not an ideal spot to have an emotionally-charged heart-to-heart. Plus all that prop food on the stage made her realize they hadn't eaten since breakfast. Swedish fish didn't really count. "Can we debrief somewhere with snacks? And a little more private? I know a great comfort food place on Christopher Street."

"Order it for delivery to the Langham. Hold the *kishkas*."

"Private *and* with a good view," Nora commented. Thirty-six stories above Manhattan, they'd warmed up with a surprisingly decent red wine from the minibar, and fueled up with butternut squash soup, crispy Brussels and just enough walnut pesto tortellini to keep them out of a carb coma. Respecting Nora's 'no subway clothes on the bed' policy, Alex had offered her one of the luxe hotel robes. "Taking back everything I said about this place." She snuggled down into the thick waffle-weave and inhaled its ginger flower scent. "Five-star is the way to go."

"I could get used to this view, too." Alex agreed, although his back was to the window. Nora, making his barely slept-in hotel bed into a nest of her own, was a welcome sight.

"Come match me."

He smiled. "Would love to. But feeling like I should shower the city off me first."

"New York has that effect on people." She gave a small shrug, the oversized robe slipping off her shoulder.

He leaned in with the wine bottle to refill the glass she held aloft, wanting to kiss that exposed skin in the process – but refrained. They had cleared the air with their apologies, but mistletoe and mezuzahs weren't the only things hanging over their heads. The metaphorical Sword of Damocles that had chased them out of bed this morning needed to be addressed before there was any climbing back in.

"So. You give all those people their first crack at Broadway."

Nora swallowed the gulp of wine she had just taken. "I do. Even if it is just thirty-minutes before the show and fifteen minutes in between acts."

"Those are important minutes." She was just as much a dream-maker as a kingmaker. "You are way more than just HR, Nora."

She had given him a true sense of the extent of People Operations at work today. "You have your hands in everything at Britesmith. And not in the way I think Hedstrom led my uncle to believe."

"He calls me his trailblazer, but what he really means is troublemaker." She pulled her robe belt tighter. "He's threatened by new ideas from others, yet he has none of his own because he is short-sighted."

Alex paced the length between the bed and the window. "Oh, I think he has ideas, they just aren't with the company's best interests in mind."

Especially now that he had a new stream of funding from Myers and Sons coming in.

"For every person I onboard, I make sure they trained to the performance level you saw today – people like Angelo, Tia. They give their best every day, and the benefits they receive here are a rarity that I think shows how much we appreciate them. Hedstrom took advantage by dipping in... and once I figured out his scheme, he's been trying to take that all away."

"How so?"

"He's been bringing in a lot of outside consultants and 1099 contract employees, especially for the satellite offices.

That's why I figured you were from Westchester or Jersey, and why I wouldn't even know you if I tripped over you at that party."

Alex smiled, thinking of that jingle bell that brought them together.

"Explain those locations to me."

"Westchester serves the venues upstate, plus Connecticut and Long Island. New Jersey extends to parts of Philadelphia. Regional theater, summer stock. Still quite large operations. But they are barely recognizable as Britesmith. More like temp staffing agencies. New York has been his bargaining chip with me. Keeping it intact if I kept his secrets. Up until now."

Nora's phone buzzed from the deep pocket of the robe. "Just Jonah, checking up on me. And calling me a total lame-ass for not coming out with them to Enclave last night." She bit back a grin, typing back.

Alex smiled. "You can totally blame that on me."

Nora kneeled on the bed and held out her phone to show him she had already said as much.

A photo popped up next, a Tree of Life menorah blazing. Blurred in the background was what appeared to be a very well-stocked bar. A large hand threw threes, in either some elaborate gang sign, Alex surmised, or to indicate what night of Hanukkah they were up to. The caption read:

Getting shamashed with my boyz!

Nora's thumb tapped to both love and quickly save the photo to her own camera roll.

"So on a scale of January to December – where do these guys fit on that calendar you bought for Sylvie?"

Nora laughed. "Jonah's like the eighteen-month version

of the *Nice Jewish Guys* calendar. The one with the bonus months you didn't know you needed. Always there for you." She slid her phone back into her pocket. "Let's see...Jay would be too busy designing, manufacturing, distributing and marketing the calendar to pose for it."

"And Avi Wolfson?"

"Avi would be the nude centerfold all the moms would steal from the middle before giving the calendar to their daughters. I'm talking pry-out-the-staples-with-their-teeth steal. He's the naughtiest nice boy you'll ever meet."

"Damn, high bar. Where would I fit in?"

Nora toyed with the belt on her robe. "That depends."

Alex dropped one knee down on the bed, then swung the other around, so he was kneeling, too. "On?"

"Are we done with the work debrief?"

"Your call."

"Good." She opened the robe. With just her bra and panties underneath, she was a vision. "That debrief is over, for now. *Your* debrief is up next, Mr. December."

Chapter Fifteen

Beck's hands slid into her robe, skimming her hips and pulling her closer. The heavy weave had trapped her body heat, and his sharp intake of breath upon touching her was indication he felt the warmth as his fingertips traveled up.

"Did your parents give you gifts every night for Hanukkah when you were a kid?" Nora asked, reveling in the way his heavy-lidded gaze took her body in.

"Yeah." His response was barely audible, as he leaned into her warmth. "Starting small..." His lips grazed her clavicle. "...then working up to a bigger and better surprise each night."

She closed her eyes, arching toward the sensation as the bulky robe fell away, helped by his hands. "Always worth the wait, right?"

"So worth it." He scooped an arm under her bottom and backed up off the bed, taking her with him. Nora squealed, no choice but to wrap her legs around him as he hauled them both in the direction of the bathroom, with its oversized rain shower.

"Naked and wet with you? Best Hanukkah ever, and we're only on the third night."

"What did he want you to do this weekend, Nora...that couldn't wait until Monday?"

It was the question Nora had been waiting for ever since they boarded the Baller. Setting pacts and hook-ups aside, she knew the real reason it had taken Beck so long to ask was that they had had to get to this moment. Here. Trust. A two-way street.

He reached into the nightstand, pulled out a crumpled sheet of 8.5 x 11 paper, and handed it to her.

Her name.

It was at the top of the list.

Along with twenty-six others. The ones she thought of every morning as she let herself get swallowed up by that building, penned into that cube ten stories up. The ones out in the wild. The ones that had been like her, with dreams she no longer had or could afford to have.

She felt her stomach drop. Nora had made it her mission to protect them, and she had failed.

"You've had this list all along?"

"I told you, I never planned to use it. From the moment I saw your name listed on the top."

"Why not? You had known me all of five minutes then."

"I've learned to spot loyalty and where it lies pretty damn quick. Remember, on the top deck? I told you – "

"How to spot your rival, and what to do about them," she finished for him.

"Exactly. And now that we know the rival of Britesmith, and of Myers and Sons, is Hedstrom...we are going to take him down."

Chapter Sixteen

Safe in Beck's arms, in their nest of hotel sheets and waffle weave, Nora finally let go.

Or maybe their nest was a net, because she had finally, fully taken that leap.

"He asked me to make some transfers between accounts before you arrived. To time it so it hit before the holiday. And to back-date some entries on the books he'd 'forgotten' about. Since letting go of Britesmith's in-house bookkeeper, he's let an outside firm handle most of the day-to-day financials, filings, AP and AR. But I've always run payroll so I've had banking privileges and access to the accounting software. I just thought he was being lazy and his usual incompetent self. He can never keep track of passwords, never gets his expense reports in on time, so it's always easier if I just go in and do what needs to be done so the outside firm can reconcile and close the books on time at month-end."

These were the things she had had to do for him. The things she wasn't proud of.

"It wasn't until he made that announcement at the

party. Then I realized he was still up to his old tricks, playing with funds, and that's why there was no bonus money."

"And that he wanted your fingers in it, your log-in on the transfer, should anything look sketchy during my first visit to the company."

"Pretty much." Hearing it come from Beck, not just her own mind perseverating on it, really sent the severity of it home.

"Did you tell anyone else?"

"I thought about asking Jonah to look things over, he's an accountant. But instead I..."

She wasn't about to mention Eli – the one who could never be summed up in a Jewish novelty calendar like her other guy friends. "...I didn't want to drag him into it. So I emailed your grandfather. Not from my work account, obviously."

"When was that?"

"It had to be early May? I had come back after bereavement leave, when Bubbe died. It was the first time I had taken any prolonged period of time off, other than random personal days here and there. And he had taken full advantage, apparently." She grimaced. "I got an Out of The Office auto-reply, but didn't feel comfortable just writing to the next person on the corporate ladder. So I wrote and mailed a letter to him instead."

"Grandpa My...he had had a fall. Around that time, and – " Beck shook his head. "He declined fast. Not his mind, that stayed sharp as a tack. But everything else – surgery, rehab, PT, only to wind up in a nursing home. Months and months of bullshit. I think he just lost the will. "I'm sorry he never..." Beck dwindled, and Nora knew just to hold him.

It wasn't until Nora was soundly asleep in his arms, that Alex was able to finish his sentence.

"I'm sorry he never got to meet you, Ruben. He would've loved you."

Chapter Seventeen

"Wow, they weren't kidding." Beck returned from answering a knock on the door, freshly-pressed suit in plastic hanging from two of his fingers. "Before start of business."

Nora smiled over the rim of her Nespresso Beck had brewed to go along with their room service breakfast. "Well, technically..."

They had been mixing business with pleasure all morning. With slightly more pleasure, then a little bit more business.

And a lot more pleasure...all before coffee.

They had spent Friday night and Saturday avoiding work talk, but now it was like they couldn't get the words out fast enough, sharing ideas, brainstorming solutions, and praising each other's thoughts on how best to bring Britesmith fully under the Myers and Sons' umbrella without losing its distinct brand, or any of its loyal employees.

Nora could barely remember the last time she had been so excited about a project. Or, sadly, the last time she felt she had a partner in anything professional or romantic. She knew these were early days, both for the company and for whatever this was between her and Beck, but she couldn't help but remain hopeful, especially as he seemed to read her thoughts.

"If we've accomplished this much in just the first four days of Hanukkah, imagine what we could do in double that time?"

She kissed him sweetly in the elevator – although the advantage of traveling thirty-six stories down afforded them some additional alone time, there were stops along the way.

"The Maccabees ain't got nothing on us," she murmured. "Well, maybe a little of that fighting spirit."

By the time they reached the lobby, they were walking off a full elevator and herding through the lobby with an early bird crowd of tourists and the random businessperson rushing to finish whatever business had brought them into town before the Christmas break.

"Depending on how this goes today...any thought to extending your trip?" Nora asked, pausing far enough away from the revolving door so as not to get swept up in the tidal wave. "The city pretty much empties out on Christmas Day itself. At least, the places where the locals are. None of this," she waved her hands to indicate Fifth Avenue, already jam-packed with people at the seven o'clock hour. "You could meet my Jew Crew...and we could catch a whole show, not just the intermission."

Beck's dimple was in full effect as he pulled her close, smiling down at her. "With you, I want the overture, the reprise, and everything in between." He stole a kiss. "The medley." Another kiss. "The curtain call." *Kiss.* "As many terms as I can remember from high school drama club so I can keep doing this."

"You forgot one." She whispered into his mouth. "A big one."

"The big standing O...vation?" His smile turned sly. "Not something I'll soon forget."

The memory of their shower together made her knees weak. "Encore, encore."

She cupped the back of his neck and caught his top lip, turning his grin into a happy sigh as she kissed him, long and hard, one final time before heading home to change for her morning commute.

"Oh, and seeing as you've got your suit back...I'm instituting Ugly Holiday Sweater Monday in the office so I can wear yours. With pride." She laughed and pushed through the revolving door before he could object.

Smiling, Alex turned to head back upstairs to suit up and gather his paperwork. Nora was zany, but exactly the right kind of zany. *My kind.* As he passed through the lobby, a slow clap of applause came from behind one of the huge pillars separating a posh seating area from the reception. But it was the voice that stopped him cold.

"Mazel, my boy. Gotta hand it to you..." His uncle came into view, shaking his head and winding down that irritating clap. "*Shtupping* on the company card may be a Myers and Sons first. Didn't think you had the balls."

"First off. I changed the room to my personal card the minute I checked in." Despite it being for business, the trip had turned very personal the minute he walked out of that office party with Nora. "And how I spend my time off is none of your business."

He continued toward the elevator, livid. And here he

thought he was only going to have to deal with one egomaniac today. This morning's dealings with Hedstrom were going to be difficult enough without Uncle Marty inserting his righteous opinions. What was he even doing here?

"Ah, but it is *my* business. Myers and Sons is *mine* now. Despite the little fool's errand my father may have assigned you to make you feel included. And we're the parent company of Britesmith. So isn't it a bit incestuous that you climbed into bed with its C-suite sweetie?"

Alex slammed his hand on the UP button and tried to school his features for a non-reaction, but could feel the vein in his temple throb. His uncle picked right up on it.

"Do you think I'm stupid? You go silent on my texts, and the next thing I know, Drew is telling me you hooked up with some hot chick on some party yacht? I was on the next flight out after Shabbat ended." He barely let a woman pushing a stroller off the lift before barreling in, continuing his tirade.

"And as if I wouldn't recognize Ms. Ruben from all the press that attracted your grandfather to this pie-in-the-sky idea in the first place. Like we need Broadway and all its drama? Thankfully, Ron has been steering the ship away from – "

"You really want to do this here?" Adrenaline surged through Alex. "Because I'd really rather get into the office and prove to you that schmuck is not steering anything – he's capsizing the whole operation."

Uncle Marty thrust a pinstriped-suited arm in front of Alex and pressed the button for the 50th floor. Of course his room was higher. The bigger the number, the better, in Martin Myers' opinion.

"The suburban offices are doing great, with practically no overhead."

Alex pushed his own button. "No, the suburban offices are basically staffed by a temp agency, and Hedstrom is dumping those fees onto New York's bottom line. He wants to get rid of the very thing that differentiates them. No loyalty, no quality. *That* is not a Myers brand."

"And you want this girl to run the show?"

"I want her to stop taking the fall for him. Tell me he put a bug in your ear about her, and I tell you how I can blow down his whole house of cards. Side with him, and... I'll still blow it down. But Myers and Sons will get dragged through the mud when he's indicted."

"So she strokes those big balls of yours and you believe any lie she tells you?" His uncle got close enough for Alex to see his nose hairs quiver. "Sit this one out, *Alexi*. Let the big boys play ball."

Pull the alarm and punch him out...or walk off and don't look back.

Alex didn't need the devil or the angel deciding his next move. He just knew he had to get to Hedstrom before his uncle did.

Despite her threat, Nora took a hard pass on the Hanukkah sweater. Well, she tried and got as far as her elbow in the sleeve. No, today had to be about maximum comfort and confidence. Beck was going to run the whole show, but she had to be ready if he needed to pull her in at any point. She was sure he probably had a baseball term for that, courtesy of his grandfather.

She folded the sweater neatly, then picked up the Do-It-Yourself Sock Monkey Kit from the coffee table to reunite it with its socks in the bedroom before contemplating her closet for the first day of a new chapter at Britesmith.

She also contemplated how different this Monday could have shaped up, had she not met the handsome stranger at the holiday work party and hijacked him for a Hanukkah hook-up on a harbor cruise.

Had she spent the weekend working.

Two Jews walk into an office Christmas party could've been the start of a lame joke. Perhaps it would be a story for them to tell for years to come, but Nora knew that was getting way ahead of herself.

For now, she was looking forward to walking into the office and sneaking a glimpse at Alex in action. Feeling that sudden bottoming out of her insides if he were to come by her cubicle. Bump into her at the water cooler. Shoot that smile at her, equally shy and seductive, the one he seemed to save for moments when she both amused and turned him on.

She pulled on her favorite pair of black Betabrand pants – they kicked ass with her suede heeled ankle boots like a boss...but allowed her movement for serenity yoga stretches if she needed to stress-bust. In solidarity with Beck, she paired it with a blazer, one with fun cuffs turned up to reveal silk pinstripes. A matching silk shell underneath kept it classy and cohesive.

She registered her phone vibrating a text against her bedspread. Then another. And another. Knowing it was a little too early for her OG Ballers group text to be blowing up, unless something was wrong, she warily reached for it.

> Change of plans. Don't come to work today. Fill you in later. Trust me.

It was odd to see such stilted words from Beck, in their text exchange pretty much exclusively full of photos.

They had agreed it was best he meet with Hedstrom one on one first. In fact, she was purposely coming in an hour late. But now, being told not to come in at all?

The second text was from Parker. As was the third. And the fourth. And the final.

Are U on way?

Tons of ppl locked out of office IDs aren't working, stuck in lobby

NORA

Where are you?!?

Chapter Eighteen

"Ah, two Meyerses for the price of one!"

Hedstrom rocked back in his desk chair. "What, did you take a jog through Central Park to get here?" He gestured to Beck's more-than-casual attire: the track pants and hooded sweatshirt he'd walked Nora to the hotel lobby in. "And to what do I owe the pleasure, Marty?"

Before his uncle could open his mouth, Alex slapped the list of names on the table. "The following people have been made redundant in the acquisition of Britesmith Hospitality Group by Myers and Sons."

Hedstrom looked at them, a calculated look of shock thinly veiling the fact that Christmas had arrived early in his mind. "Okay..." he began to tap at his keyboard. "You sure you don't want me to have my People Operations girl handle the paperwork?"

"Seeing as my uncle disabled *your girl's* building access this morning, that may prove difficult."

He had beaten Marty to the turnstiles that morning, thanks to having skipped shaving and suiting up. Only to have his uncle flash his company credentials, and bark orders at Security. It actually worked out better for Alex's plan to keep Nora as far away from the office as possible. Knowing what he knew about her, the hasty text he sent her would not fly. But he'd hoped its last two words would resonate with her.

"I knew you'd see the light, son." Marty tapped his temple. "Numbers."

Alex walked over to the grimy window of Hedstrom's corner office. The one spot on the floor that actually had a view, yet the filth and neglect barely let the light in. But Alex knew – Nora's people were all out there, living their lives, planning their dreams. Their auditions, like April and Tommy. Their weddings, like Tia. And their retirement, like Angelo.

"Grandpa My would never have treated people like a number and you know that."

"But he knew numbers mattered."

Alex turned to face his uncle. "*Stats* matter. And like in baseball, you have to be looking at the right stats."

"*Ach.* You sound just like him, you know."

"And that's such a bad thing?"

His uncle's face softened; for just a moment Alex saw a striking resemblance. Not only to Grandpa My. But something he saw in his own face, every day when he glanced in the mirror.

Uncle Marty was looking for a sign.

How many summer evenings had Hal Myers probably spent out on the back lawn, teaching first his son, then his grandsons, the art of throwing a ball? Passing along, from generation to generation, the silent, subtle back-and-forth between pitcher and catcher to communicate what was about to go down.

His uncle's brow raised, perhaps not fully understanding, but at least open to the play. Trusting Alex for once.

"And...done." Hedstrom made one last keystroke with a flourish. "Been looking to trim the fat for a while now." He printed the status list from the HR software, strode to the printer and handed it to Alex.

"Congratulations, Hedstrom – you just laid off over forty percent of your staff, immediately triggering a partial termination of Britesmith's 401(k) retirement plan."

Hedstrom frowned, looking confused. Then – a glimmer of panic set in.

Score one for Team Hayseed.

"That's right, *Ron.* You just fully vested all these employees. They are entitled to any employer contribution being made up to this point. You *have* been making your *employer* contributions into a trust, right? Assuming it's just your employees you steal from?"

"How dare you accuse me – I'm the goddamn CEO, you SOB!"

"Yeah, well, here are some more acronyms for you. ERISA, The Employee Retirement Security Act of 1974 which you breached when you misused your employee's retirement funds." Hedstrom had no poker face, but his ugly mug went as white as a playing card. "EBSA, DOL, IRS, and the Myers BOD," Alex ticked off, starting to enjoy himself. "All would be very interested in hearing all this. Shall I go on?"

"I've heard enough." Marty stepped up to bat now. "Ron, step down. Immediately. And I'm sure the Board of Directors will agree when they convene at nine o'clock Central Time on my behest. We'll issue a press release, you keep your reputation, but you can slink down into the hole you came from. Far away from anything attached to the

Myers name. Security will escort you out." He reached for the CEO's desk phone.

Hedstrom gave them both a long, hateful stare. Then turned to his keyboard once again. *Don't mess with Iowa,* Alex thought triumphantly. *Score two.*

The printer across the room whirred again. "Bring it to me, I'll sign it," Hedstrom grunted. No sooner had Alex turned his back did Hedstrom attack the keyboard with renewed fervor. Paused, swore, and manically typed some more. "That bitch!"

"Oh yeah, and if you were thinking of making any last-minute transfers yourself...you're about eleven hours too late." Nora had reset not only new banking passwords last night, but a two-signer verification for anyone trying to move money internally or externally. "Since you're in the habit of forgetting passwords...don't bother trying to remember your old one. It no longer works."

"IT will help speed all that along," Marty added. "I called them, too." Obviously not his first rodeo when it came to terminations, but Alex was impressed by his uncle's about-face. *Bases officially loaded.*

But there was still more damage control to do.

"Grand slam on the grand scam, kid." Uncle Marty praised. "Now go run us home, rookie."

"Parker!"

Nora's assistant was running interference from behind the main turnstiles separating the prohibited from the permitted. The security guards – guys she had known for years, whom she greeted with a hello and a smile every day

– looked both apologetic and fed up as Britesmithers tried, and failed, to swipe in.

"This. Is. Bananas!" Parker hollered to her, dodging the sea of other building occupants as they streamed in to start their work day.

This is the moment of truth, she thought, pulling her own ID from her purse.

"Hang on, people." Charlie, the head of security, just hung up his phone. "All of you all, you've been called to the conference room on the Mezzanine level. Not you, Ruben." He held up a copy of the same printed list Beck had shown her yesterday. Sure enough, her name on the top was crossed off.

"Nora, is it true?" Tia strode right up to her. The wide Covergirl smile she usually flashed so easily for Nora was pulled tight in a grim, lipsticked line. "Losing a bonus I can handle. But this? Joshua and I are trying to get a mortgage! Can't do that on one income."

"Wait, what?" Nora needed a beat; this was not what she and Beck had discussed.

After all they had shared, and all she had confided in him...had he just gone ahead and done the thing he had come to town to do in the first place?

His so-called "change of plans" ...was really no change at all. With one exception: if her name was crossed off the list, she had somehow managed to sacrifice all of her staff in the process of saving herself.

"Tia, I swear I'm going to figure this out." It wasn't just one upset and disappointed face she was assuring. As each of her staff filed by, on their way up to the mezzanine, she heard herself promising each and every one. Whether they heard her – or believed her – was another story.

"Yeah, right. Merry Christmas to us," Fran from

Marketing kvetched. "Don't bother, Nora." Two of the staffers from yesterday's rock opera, girls who pulled double-duty on the show's dark days as social media coordinators, gave Nora their best resting bitch faces as they marched behind her.

And at the back of the line was April. She wouldn't even look at Nora.

Parker had come through the turnstile to stand with her, but she could see the conflicted look on her poor assistant's face. He raised a fist in solidarity to his colleagues. "What the actual fuck is going on?" he asked. "Christmas Eve-Eve is supposed to be about me and you sneaking bites of Maureen's leftover yule log from the Sales Department fridge and doing as little work as possible."

He was right, it was traditionally a coast on auto-pilot day...not an HR nightmare. "Have you seen Hedstrom today?"

"Yeah, he was in his office when I got in. Totally felt like business as usual. Then April texted to say she was coming from the coffee shop with a big order for us, so I came down to help her carry. Next thing I know, there's this guy in a suit coming in, acting all hot shit and telling security not to let Britesmith staff upstairs, least of all, you. "

Nora felt sick to her stomach. *Trust me.* How many times had Beck said that?

"And that's when I texted you. Angelo was the first to arrive."

Hearing that hurt her heart – Britesmith's oldest employee loved coming to the voluntary Monday All Hands meetings Nora had instituted last year. It was a time for any employee to gather and discuss industry insights, learn of show openings and closings, and share ideas. To think of him being turned away...

Nora contemplated the Security Desk. Then the turnstile. She hadn't jumped over one since she was thirteen and Vivi Rosenthal had shaken her down for her MetroCard at the 72nd Street subway line after Hebrew school.

"I believe in those pants – slay queen." Parker encouraged. "I'll even hold your boots."

Nora leaned on the security guard's desk. "You know what I'm thinking and I know what you're thinking." Charlie smirked, held down the access button and glanced the other way. She grabbed the list and she and Parker scurried into an open elevator. Its door sliding shut with a chime that her assistant's phone echoed.

"Holy crap, Nolan just texted. IT was called in to confiscate Hedstrom's laptop."

Chapter Nineteen

The tenth floor was eerily quiet. Someone had left their desk fan on, which blew against a long strand of silver tinsel decorating a cubicle; it danced and died, danced and died, each time the fan oscillated. But that was the only movement down the long corridor to Hedstrom's office.

Parker ducked into his cube, no doubt eager to jump on Britesmith's messaging platform for any further intel.

The fluorescent lights auto-clicked on as Nora passed each cubicle. An energy-saving function for when sections of the floor were left unstaffed. She wondered if the office would ever return to fully lit again.

Too lit to quit. Good thing she hadn't worn Beck's ugly Hanukkah sweater. It couldn't be further from the truth. After the adrenaline surge came the shaky, jangly feeling. Her hand shook as she stopped and grabbed a pen, scrawling letters to form words on the back of the fateful slip of paper containing the list.

She couldn't believe she had been entertaining fantasies about a flirty, office romance just this morning. The excitement and thrill she had imagined of glimpsing Beck at work had been replaced by dread. And pent-up rage. Had she literally traded in one boss on a power trip for another? At least with Hedstrom, his motivations were pretty much in plain sight. Worse with Beck, because she had let herself believe – trust – that they were in this together.

Hedstrom's chair was empty, but it had a suitcoat slung over the back of it. Jay and Avi's voices rose up in her ears, questioning her about Beck on the Baller. *What's he want from you? What's he expecting?* She should've thrown the jacket – and the thought of hooking up with its owner – overboard that night and just stayed in the safe company of her friends, people who had her best interests at heart.

Desk drawers were open and paper was strewn. A thick, blue file folder sat open in the middle of the desk. Beck must've found it exactly where she had told him it would be, and he must've used it exactly how she had instructed. Because even Hedstrom had a confidential personnel file where she kept track of things, and also kept his contract. His non-compete clause. And now, she could see as she stepped closer, it held his signed resignation letter.

At least Beck did the one thing he said he would do.

"Young lady."

She turned to find an older man at the window. Sleeves rolled but tie intact. His dress pants belonged to the jacket, which she now noticed had pinstripes, like her own.

Not Beck's.

"I wish we were meeting under better circumstances," the man began, "and that my nephew – "

"*I* wish I had never met him. And it doesn't matter which Myers family member I tell this to." Her words came out in a rush, as she smacked the paper down. "I quit."

And without another word to spare, Nora stormed out.

Alex Beckman stood in the entryway. Not even trying to blend in this time.

The conference room was back to its regular corporate landscape; the only trace of the holiday party was a skid-mark of faux snow on the nylon carpet that the janitor must've missed while vacuuming.

He glanced at the ceiling. No mistletoe.

Turning his gaze to the twenty-six expectant faces, he found they had all fallen silent when he walked in. No more dirty dancing elves or drink-slinging Mrs. Clauses. The karaoke girls were silent and the guys were stone sober.

He realized how he must've looked to them – loosely laced running shoes, college sweatshirt, and a shadow of a beard that had clearly seen three five o'clocks already. Not exactly like the representative of a parent company.

But that was okay.

"I know I met some of you at Friday's party, although that didn't exactly show me what you do on a daily basis. Luckily, I had Nora Ruben as my tour guide this weekend. She took me into some your venues to give me a sense of the enormous effort you give and the pride you take in what you do. Now, I know change is never easy, but please hear me out..."

Chapter Twenty

"It's a dark day."

"Darling, aren't you being a bit dramatic? Jobs come and go. Boys come and go."

"I mean, on Broadway, Mom. Dark curtain...a day off?"

"I don't remember your grandmother ever having one of *those*."

Nora had just rage-quit her job – was there some sort of app for rage-quitting a call, short of smashing your phone on the floor? Her mother was the last person she felt like talking to, let alone explaining the past three days.

"Anyway, chin up. Tomorrow's a new day."

"No, tomorrow is Christmas Eve." She had already called in every favor to give her staff – no, no longer hers, *Britesmith's* staff – that day off, and then it was Christmas. Come December 26th, as the lights of Broadway clicked back on, would there be anyone to continue fulfilling the company's contracts?

At least Hedstrom had attempted business as usual while hell-bent on running the company under. Myers and Sons didn't have a clue – Broadway wasn't baseball; it didn't get called when it started to rain. And New York wasn't Des Moines. There was a reason it was called the city that never slept.

Whatever.

No longer my circus, Nora reminded herself. *No longer my monkeys.*

No, her monkey sat in front of her, legs half-sewn.

Which was the reason she had had to call her mother in the first place.

"Can you just tell me where you moved Bubbe's extra sewing supplies?"

Some people might drown their sorrows by binge-watching bad shows or in a bottle of booze. In times of trouble, Nora found herself turning to the bobbin.

Besides her Chai necklace, Nora's other enduring gift from her grandmother had been her Singer sewing machine. But it was a 1970s industrial beast that she had no room in her own apartment for, and so heavy, she would've had to hire a moving crew. So it still resided where Bubbe had resided up until the end: the extra bedroom of her parent's Lenox Hill apartment. The room her mother had wasted no time turning into the exercise room she'd always coveted.

Her mother sighed. "Check the closet. Top shelf. Suzie might have moved it."

Suzie was also probably responsible for the bird's nest of tangled thread Nora had discovered under the machine's needle plate, as the family housekeeper was the only other person besides Nora who knew how to use the machine. And not nearly as careful with the family heirloom.

"Thanks, Mom."

Sure enough, Ruth Ruben had been right about something. There, between her mother's yoga mats and kettle bells, sat Bubbe's sewing basket. Extra bobbins, carefully-kept quality threads in every color, new needles – everything she could possibly need to solve the problem at hand.

If only she had Bubbe. And her sage advice.

Tears fell on the half-monkey/half-still-socks with the Rockford Original Red Heel. Wiping her eyes, she began the methodical steps to correct the tension of the machine, and within herself.

Smoothing fabric under the gentle hum of the machine, she could practically hear her grandmother's voice, creating a new mantra for her current state.

Be kind to yourself.

Do things from a place of love.

You are not your job.

And as for Beck?

Her mother had been right about one other thing: It was just as easy to fall for a Jewish man. And it hurt like hell.

Also, fuck Eli and his wisdom – there had been no net waiting for her.

"What do you mean, quit?"

Alex had spent the better part of the day in one-on-ones, trying to meet with as many of the New York staff possible, while his uncle had made closed-door calls to the board, shareholders and Myers and Sons attorneys. Nora had never been far from his mind the whole time – especially as each Britesmither's story was more enlightening than the one before it. When the time had come to speak with Parker, Alex found her assistant skulking in an empty cubicle, stuffing his face with some sort of crumbly chocolate cake smeared with whipped cream.

"Read the room. Or rather, the cubicle." The guy said

miserably. "*Her* cubicle." He gestured to the mainly bare fabric walls, where Alex could only imagine Nora had hung pictures of her Jew Crew to keep her company while she worked. There was a plant in the corner on its last green leaf, but she had told him she had a black thumb when it came to keeping anything green alive.

She had told him a lot in the short time they had known each other.

"She even took the plastic menorah I gave her so she would know the true joy of tacky holiday kitsch," he bemoaned over a mouthful. "*And* I'm stuck eating yule log by myself."

"Is that Maureen's, from Sales?"

Parker nodded. "So bad, yet you find yourself craving it once a year." He offered his plate to Alex.

"It tastes like if sawdust and Cool-Whip had a baby."

Parker raised his brow, head bobbing somberly to one side. "Swaddled in a blanket of bittersweet cocoa and regret."

Fair assessment. The two men traded the plate back and forth until only a pile of crumbs remained. "She didn't even say goodbye."

Fuck. This hadn't been part of the plan.

Then again, they had only made a plan A. Removing Hedstrom from the equation.

Plan B had come to him last night, when he couldn't sleep.

He had held her, watched her as she slept. Her hair like an inky waterfall on the pillow, then spilling against his chest when she tossed and turned. She touched her necklace, even while dreaming.

His grandfather's words had tunneled down to a singular focus: *Take care of Nora.*

Cutting out the cancer that had been Hedstrom's mismanagement and deceit was a start. But he couldn't very well leave her to deal with the fallout of a company that had been declining for years.

Quietly, he had slipped out of bed. Angled his laptop so the light wouldn't disturb her. Postponed his Tuesday flight. And had begun to research.

He thought he'd figured everything out. A way to give Nora the epic story she deserved, come Monday morning.

But had he just lost her in the process?

"How could you let her just walk in here and quit? Why didn't you call me back upstairs? I would've explained everything to her!"

For once, his uncle didn't go on the defensive or try to refute. In fact, he was sitting so still, one hand up to his brow as he leaned on the desk, that Alex thought for a second he was asleep. Then Marty's shoulders began to shake.

"I'm sorry, Alex. I didn't know."

His uncle clutched an envelope in his hands. He slowly held it out before pulling back slightly. Like he wanted to get something off his chest, but at the same time didn't want to let go of what was troubling him just yet.

"I've lived so long under the shadow of a great man." He whispered the words again. "I didn't know."

Alex took the envelope, and everything hit him all at once. The handwriting. The stamp. The postmark date.

Now he knew why Nora's name had sounded so familiar at first. Way before he saw it on some list. His grandfather *had* replied to her. And Alex had mailed the goddamn letter to her himself.

He remembered the afternoon in technicolor heartbreak. His grandfather had tasked him with three things that day: find a stamp, mail a letter, and buy his mother a birthday card. One final card from her dying father. The last task was so out-of-body sad and surreal, he had done the other two "minor" tasks on auto-pilot. Now he realized, not minor at all.

"Was it open?" He asked his uncle, who shook his head.

"The lawyers had advised me to go through all of Hedstrom's correspondence, and there was plenty. Even in this day and age of supposedly paperless communication. He had stacks of unopened mail. Past-due bills, customer service inquiries, even potential clients reaching out. That letter was mixed in."

Now the envelope was neatly opened across the top, and a letter opener sat on the desk amid scattered papers. Alex could imagine his uncle's shock at seeing his own father's handwriting amidst the impersonal typed business envelopes. And his eagerness to discover what was inside.

"She was already gone when I found it, Alexi."

"Well then. I have to find her."

Chapter Twenty-One

> Question: do you have a honey bear at your place? I only need a drizzle from him.

Nora had decided she was going to drink her feelings, courtesy of Angelo's recipe. Or maybe in homage to him.

She had whip-stitched and slip-stitched until her fingers were numb. It turned out that angrily stuffing batting into a sock monkey torso was oddly gratifying. But she had stopped short of finishing when she got to the face. It was up to the creator whether this creature would go through life with a permanent frown or a smile on his little red-heeled face, and Nora wasn't quite ready to play God like that. It had been a day.

Hence. A drink.

Talia's response was almost immediate. *It's on its way.* Bless her best friend, whose catering business was busy as hell, especially around the holidays, but always stocked with supplies and had a plethora of delivery people at the ready.

Nora shared her location, even though she suspected Talia had probably already checked her app.

Her parents had bourbon and, weirdly enough, orange marmalade in their fridge. She was just trying to figure out if the liquor store down the street would deliver the rest of the ingredients she needed when the buzzer rang.

"Papa Bear, with your honey."

Nora's spirits lifted. Talia hadn't said she was sending it special delivery.

Jonah appeared in the hallway a few seconds later. Sure enough, with a plastic honey bear container in his hand. She ran to meet him in her socks, throwing her arms around her old friend.

"Easy now, Papa Bear had a rough night. Too many of those Challah-day Hangovers. Hey...hey now, why the tears?"

"I quit today. Before Beck could fire me."

"Wait, what? Suit guy?" Jonah flopped onto her parents' sectional, taking up half the thing. Nora felt a wave of nostalgia and gratitude. When he was first looking for an accounting job out of college, Jonah would crash at her parents' place the night before early morning interviews in the city. They took to him like the son they never had. "Hold on. Avi is texting me."

"Tell him to bring cherry liqueur and chocolate bitters." She curled up at his side, honey bear clutched to her chest.

"*Bring...cherry...liqueur...*" he recited as he texted. "I think I just threw up in my mouth a little. He'll be here in fifteen. Can I have some tea with that honey bear? I'll trade you some sympathy for it."

His request reminded her of joking around with Beck in her kitchen. How he took his sugar with coffee and cream. *God, how could that have only been thirty-six hours ago?*

She felt like she could sleep for the next thirty-six. That would be ideal. Maybe Talia would even trade in their standing date with Chinese food and a movie on Christmas and have her over for a slumber party. Nora could help her grate onions for the Katz family eighth night holiday dinner, so she wouldn't have to make any excuses for her tears.

"I can't believe I let my guard down, Jo."

She pushed herself up and went to put on the kettle, saying no more. She knew she'd only have to repeat things after she buzzed Avi up.

Please Nora – I can explain everything

It's not how you think

I'm sorry things got so complicated

Why was she even torturing herself by reading Beck's texts? Things seemed pretty cut and dry, no explanation needed. He had come to town to cut Britesmith's staff in half. Mission accomplished. He and his uncle could go toast themselves in the hotel bar, or jump off the roof for all she cared. At least he was leaving tomorrow, leaving whatever mess behind.

After Christmas, she would reach out to each employee and see if she could help with job placement. Not as a superior, but as a friend. They'd be sure to get snatched up in a heartbeat by any number of Britesmith's competitors, given their training. Maybe she would even offer herself up to one of those companies, too, once her non-compete clause was through.

Or maybe it was time for a re-invention.

Her fingers, achy from their sewing marathon, throbbed. But in a good way; as if to remind her there was more to life than Britesmith.

"Why has every night of Hanukkah involved copious amounts of alcohol?" Avi blew in, dark hair down and disheveled from the wind. When he shed his leather coat, a wave of tequila came off him.

"Why is this night different from all other nights?" Jonah injected a bit of Passover humor. "*Ma Nishtana*, my friend." He gratefully accepted the mug Nora handed him; dwarfed in his hands despite its oversize, then proceeded to hemorrhage half the honey bear into his tea.

"Take." Avi handed her the paper bag of requested ingredients.

"Where's Sylvie?"

Nora swore his pupils dilated at the mention of her name, but he merely shrugged, kicking off his shoes.

"Think it's just us, Talia and Jay were doing a thing today," Jonah supplied.

"I take it neither of you will Drink Your Feelings with me?"

"Maybe a sip. Hair of the dog. Asher's Bar crushed us last night." Avi made himself right at home, helping himself to a big glass of water from the built-in on the Rubens' fancy fridge.

What a thousand adoring fans wouldn't give to see their idol like this: standing in the kitchen with a hole in his sock, and chewing crushed ice. Nora couldn't help thinking she was the luckiest girl in the world. But that wasn't the reason why.

Avi proceeded to raid her parent's china cabinet while she fetched the bourbon from the liquor cabinet. "Candles?"

He held her childhood Winnie the Pooh menorah aloft.

That's right. It was still Hanukkah. Only the fourth night.

And no one should light the candles alone.

Alex stood under the giant menorah in Central Park, but his head and heart were miles away.

Actually, just blocks away.

His texts to Nora had gone unanswered. Phone calls, straight to voicemail. He'd even gone to her apartment, but she didn't answer the buzzer. Defeated, he headed back to Britesmith's office, where at least he could bury himself in work.

As much as Marty's arrival had complicated things, Alex was glad his uncle was there, and finally acting like a mentor. Ever since he had opened that letter, the man seemed more humbled and at peace. They'd gone to the candle-lighting together; Alex leading the way this time, no longer feeling so much like a tourist in this town.

Like the lay-off list of the New York 27 he'd carried earlier, Grandpa My's written response to Nora's report of Hedstrom's misdeeds burned a hole in his pocket, unread by him. Whatever it said, it was Nora's to read first. Or perhaps they could read it together.

Meet me at the menorah?

A memory flashed as he texted her again, her voice

echoing in his ear. The excitement, the chase, the tease, the promise of that night on the boat.

Back when all they had bargained for was one night.

He'd written, and he had waited. Now, he stood apart as the crowd cheered the fourth candle being lit. His own words from this morning in the elevator echoing back:

Imagine what we could do in double that time?

He wasn't going to give up without a fight.

I'll be here waiting every night till the 8th night, Nora. Please say you'll come. I have something for you.

Chapter Twenty-Two

For once, Nora hadn't been overwhelmed with the holiday time. In fact, she had been relieved to sit back and let Christmas take hold of everyone, all around her. It provided the perfect excuse to stay in pajamas, sew, and binge all the shows all day. In the evenings, she got in cuddle time with her Year Course crew, had perfected a version of Drink Your Feelings that Angelo would be proud of, and got to spend quality time with Talia over mounds of sesame noodles from Ollie's and a chick flick. It was sorely needed soul-restoration for the two of them to play catch-up and commiserate on being single in the city.

As she lit candles five, six and seven however, she couldn't avoid thinking of Beck. And his latest string of text messages.

I waited under the seventh candle for you.

Did you know the 7th inning stretch supposedly originated when President Taft attended a baseball game? He got up to stretch and everyone thought he was leaving so they stood out of respect, and it became a tradition.

Baseball games usually start around 7 minutes after 7pm, so the networks can get an extra commercial or two in while they have everyone's attention.

Rennie Stennett of the Pirates is the only batter in modern history to ever go for a perfect 7-for-7 hits in a game. Sadly it was against the Cubs!

Most baseball series, including the World Series, are played best-of-7. Usually they don't need all 7 games. But it sure is exciting when they do.

Happy 7th night, Nora.

She honestly didn't know what to think. He'd upended her career, and still had time to share baseball stats with her?

One thing she did know – the hiatus from work made her realize she had been veering toward major burnout. Her ADHD hyper-focusing combined with the constant chaos Hedstrom had subjected her to had been a perfect storm, and not good for her at all.

Beck's suggestion about not really knowing what's best for someone, or even yourself at times, kept re-surfacing. Something her mind turned over and excavated as she finished sewing. New Jocko had his eyes now, and a tail.

Britesmith wasn't a ham sandwich on sesame seed bread. It wasn't life or death.

But it also was more than an cheap itchy sweater you could just toss aside.

Sometimes you just have to approach it together and figure it out...the hard way.

It hurt that he had gone ahead and made decisions without her. But at the end of the day, it was his family's company.

And as for the two of them? She still didn't know if she believed in soulmates, or even the concept of *bashert*. They'd agreed to one night, and maybe he had had other intentions. But she was able to see the good in what they briefly had.

She carefully backstitched Jocko a mouth, slightly upturned.

It could pass for a smile.

Chapter Twenty-Three

"Nora! Yay! You came!"

Parker, fresh off the catwalk, positively glowed. It was his first year participating in the Broadway Cares/Equity Fights AIDS' *Now We Don Our Gay Apparel* charity fashion show, although he and Nolan always volunteered for the annual event. It took place the Friday afternoon after Christmas every year and she made sure to approve their time off requests since they worked so hard on it, but had never attended herself due to work.

No problem with that now.

"And you brought me paparazzi." He smacked red lacquered nails to his chest, truly *verklempt*. "Way better than flowers! Hi!"

"My good friend, Sylvie. Sylvie, this is Parker."

"Mister Heat Miser to you, young lady." He patted his spiky red wig, striking a pose for her.

"I got some great action shots of you up there. Nora will send them to you, promise." She squeezed Nora's shoulder. "I want to shoot the next designer, he's a Back Bay Boston boy. See you out at Talia and Jay's parents' house tonight? Later, hot stuff."

Parker caught the kiss she blew, then wiped his face of any trace of merriment. "I ate nearly an entire Yule log on your behalf, you know. They almost didn't let me on the runway."

"Oh please." She glanced around the venue. Usually, whichever theater had a show closing by New Year's offered up a matinee slot. This year it happened to be one of their regular contracts. Although, to her dismay, she didn't recognize a single staffer.

"I guess that's the way it's gonna be now, huh?" She nodded toward concessions.

"Yeah." Parker held up a hand and smiled at the guy behind the counter. "The Bridge and Tunnel guys really saved the day. After Beck, of course."

"He's moved the temp staff in?"

"Only this week, to give the New York office a breather during the transition. You should've seen the hug Tia laid on him."

"Tia? I've been trying to get a hold of her. April, too. I still think I can help them find work –"

Parker shook his head, flaming hair and all.

"They will have plenty of work with the new Myers contracts, Nora."

Nora had to wrap her head around what he was laying down a mile a minute. "Wait, but – all those Britesmith layoffs...it was all...?"

"It was all to protect the employee's investments, and to make sure Britesmith paid what the employees were owed. Nolan was nearby for the whole thing when it went down. Said Beck was a total rock star." Parker pulled his huge wig off, holding it under his arm. "Nora, the layoffs caused them all to become immediately vested in the old retirement plan. Beck had figured it out. He kept Hedstrom on the hook just long enough to trigger it."

"Old plan?"

"Sure, everyone's all under the parent company now. We all Team Hayseed, baby! On their payroll, benefits, everything." He did a flossing move in his Christmas couture. "It never made sense to keep everything siloed. This helps with overhead while also presenting a more cohesive brand."

"Um, who even are you with this lingo?"

"I'm still POO number two. Which sounds terrible, so we are changing the title. But I report to someone in Des Moines now."

Nora felt a tiny stab of sadness, guilt and... something else unidentifiable, but it felt a bit like joy bursting in her chest.

Her people were safe. They were being taken care of. No longer by her, but...

"Take care of yourself." Parker hugged her long and hard, his spiky wig in his hand poking her. "I gotta go. Oh, and Nora? Happy last night of Hanukkah."

Alex nodded and smiled as people said hello and Happy Hanukkah. After four nights of gathering to watch the communal lighting, their faces were beginning to look familiar to him, so he guessed his was, too.

Who would've thought, in a place as big as New York?

It was still light out, just before sundown on the final night of Hanukkah. It was his last full day in the city for a while, and he wanted to drink it all in.

Uncle Marty had left on Christmas Day, after taking Alex and Drew out for lunch at a kosher Chinese place where they were able to order a matzo ball soup and an egg roll at the same meal. New York was full of tiny miracles.

Nora was right, the city had emptied out on Christmas. He thought maybe he'd have a better chance of finding her without the crowds. But instead, he found himself wandering neighborhoods he'd never been to before.

Places he could maybe see himself living someday.

Maybe.

Alex checked his watch, then settled on a bench. He pulled out the letter he had been carrying for the last four days. Even if Nora wasn't coming, he still had this last piece of his grandfather, and her to thank for it.

Dusk was settling, heightening the crowd's murmur of growing excitement. There were still twinkling white lights everywhere he looked – from the horse carriages lining the street to the trees in front of The Plaza, to the glittering skyscrapers stretched out beyond him. It was as if everyone wanted to prolong the magic of both holidays for a little while longer.

A flashing caught his eye in the distance.

All the Christmas camouflage in the world couldn't hide her.

"Hey, Beckman."

The blinking was coming from the stunner in blue and black – or rather, the tacky black sweater she wore with CHAI MAINTENANCE surrounded in blue lights.

"Hey, Ruben. You're early." He stood.

Nora looked up at the menorah, back at him, and shook her head. "I'm not, actually. I'm four nights late. I should've been here on Monday to hear you out."

"And I never should've left you out of the loop to begin with. I'm sorry."

She let him envelop her. He buried his nose in her hair, reveling in the way it held the cool night air. Breathing her in like he had the scents of the city all week without her. It was sensory overload, but in the best way.

"It actually turned out to be the best thing for me, honestly. Even if we didn't know it at the time. And didn't figure it out together. I think I had some things to figure out about myself, too. Quitting helped me do that."

"Good thing I didn't fire you when I had the chance," he wisecracked.

She bumped the back of his knees with her bag. "Brought you something."

"Twenty-dollars-in-twenty-minutes-something?"

"No, I'm a great re-gifter. It's one thing you'll learn about me."

He wanted to learn all the things. But would settle for one thing at a time.

She sat down on the bench. Patted the spot next to her. Then plunked the bag in his lap.

"It's not a bomb, is it? It's blinking."

"Shhh, go on."

He pulled out a pleasantly plump sock monkey, classic in looks. Sure enough, his little hat had the bell on it.

And he wore the ugliest sock-monkey-sized Hanukkah sweater.

"I figured you weren't going to be wearing it again," she shrugged. "So I tailored it. To fit him. Think he'll fit in back in Des Moines?"

"Oh Jocko 2.0 was born to be a hayseed." He slid the creation back into the bag. "But also kind of a city slicker, too. I think he'll fit in here as well."

There was that secret Nora smile. God, he had missed everything about her.

"So. Parker told me everything," she began.

"Well, not everything. I'm getting rid of the old building space."

"Oh?" She turned to him. "Moving to where the sky's a little lower?"

"To Times Square, actually. A little closer to the action. Open floor plan, lots of windows." *Maybe room for a piano.* "Not a cubicle in sight. For Myers and Sons' new division."

Nora was quiet, fiddling with the strings on the bag. He wondered what she was thinking.

"Nice sweater." He nudged her.

She grinned. "Just embracing my true self. Learning my strengths and weaknesses."

"Ah, strengths and weakness. Classic MBA application questions. Good for job interviews, too. You're hired, by the way. To head up the new division if you want to."

"And what would that be?"

"I'm calling it Costuming and Hospitality Arts, Inc."

"The *CHAI* division?"

He smirked. "It kind of just worked out that way, yeah. I told my uncle what you showed me on Broadway. He loved it — the integration and immersion of customer service into the show and tailoring the concessions based on the show theme. Truly an art. You'd have your twenty-six staff back – to start with. And Myers and Sons will handle all the admin, so you can focus on the creative stuff."

"What do you think your Grandpa My would say?"

"Well, funny you should ask..." He handed her the letter. "A gift for you. Took a bit longer than twenty minutes to find it."

"And priceless." Nora's eyes widened. "Have you read it?"

He shook his head. "You first."

"No. Together."

Dear Ms. Ruben - Officer of the People:

Thank you for your letter, and I apologize I am only responding now. I'll keep this short, because I know you are very busy. And because - how do I put this? I'm short on time as well.

My family doesn't want to hear it, but in terms of certain things in life – good or bad – when you know, you know. I've been seeing my Leah in my dreams, and for once I don't mind that I am sleeping more than I'm awake - not when my bashert is waiting patiently for me.

(Young lady if you don't know the term bashert I suggest you look it up on your Google.)

Because love is the most important thing in the world - but baseball is pretty good, too. I learned that from the great Yogi Berra.

The situation you describe is troubling. It

was brave and bold of you to write. Rest assured, I am sending my grandson Alex to New York, to help you with it. He'll know what to do.

Please just be patient, as there are a few things he needs to do here in the meantime. (First off, he needs to find me a stamp and to mail this letter.)

Thank you for caring about the future of Myers and Sons. For us.

Hal Myers

Beck wiped his eyes with his coat sleeve and took a shaky breath. But he was smiling, and hadn't let go of her hand for a second.

"Looks like he had a little advice for you after all."

"For us," she echoed, leaning up for a kiss. He dropped one, full of hope and promise, gently on her lips and Nora felt a burst of joy ignite. Or maybe it was the eight candles behind them, finally illuminated in all their glory.

"Want to get out of here?" she suggested. "It's not quite the Baller, but I know of a great eighth night party."

He was pretty cute, for a Hayseed.

"Lead the way."

Love the OG Matzo Ballers? Get Talia's story **The Dreidel Do-Over** *by my writer BFF, Amanda Usen! Learn how Jay's "secret weapon" sister pulled off all sorts of miracles on the ship, and more*

Wondering what's next for the Matzo Baller series? Watch for **The Rugelach Road Trip** (Avi) and **The Menorah Matchmaker** (Jay), releasing Hanukkah 2024!

Also by Jessica Topper

The "Love & Steel" series:

Louder Than Love

Deeper Than Dreams

Softer Than Steel

More Than Merry

The "Much 'I Do' About Nothing" series:

Dictatorship of the Dress

Courtship of The Cake

The "Matzo Ballers Hanukkah Romance" series:

The Hanukkah Hook-Up (*Jessica Topper*)

The Dreidel Do-Over (*Amanda Usen*)

The Menorah Matchmaker (*Amanda Usen*)

The Rugelach Road Trip (Jessica Topper)

Sign up for Jessica's newsletter for exclusive content, news, giveaways and more!

https://jesstopper.com

About the Author

Jessica Topper has been in love with the beauty of the written word ever since she memorized Maurice Sendak's Chicken Soup with Rice at the age of three.

After earning a B.A. in English Literature and her Master's Degree in Library Science, Jessica went on to work as a librarian in New York City before trading in the books for bookkeeping. For seventeen years, she worked in the production office of an international touring rock band.

Jessica broke the rock romance mold with her 2013 debut novel LOUDER THAN LOVE. Her follow-up romantic comedy, DICTATORSHIP OF THE DRESS, was named one of Publishers Weekly's Best Books of 2015.

She lives in Western New York with her family - including two cats that love to walk across her keyboard. Visit her online at jessicatopper.com

Glossary

Adonai: God
B&T: Bridge and Tunnel - derogatory term for people who live in the suburbs or boroughs outside of Manhattan
Bar/Bat Mitzvah: translates to "son/daughter of the commandment"
Baruch atah Adonai: "Praised By Thou Oh Lord our God" - every Jewish prayer pretty much begins with this
Bashert: "meant to be" - especially for relationships, soul-mates etc
Bimah: raised platform in a temple where the Torah is read
Blini: pancake or crepe - Russian or Eastern European in origin
***Blintz*:** rolled crepe, typically filled with cheese or fruit
Boychik: young man - term of endearment
Bubbaleh: term of endearment - like sweetie, darling
Bubbe: Grandmother
Buñuelos: Sephardic donuts served at Hanukkah
Chai: Hebrew word for "life", recognizable 2-letter symbol for luck

Chuppah: Jewish wedding canopy, can be freestanding like a trellis but traditionally held up by poles by close friends
Dreidel: 4-sided top, played during Hanukkah - means "to turn"
Gelt: chocolate coins, wrapped in gold foil
Halva/halvah: Middle Eastern dessert, fudge-like in texture, usually made with tahini (sesame paste), sugar, spices and nuts
Hanukkiah: another word for menorah
Hava Nagila: traditional Jewish folk song, celebratory
Hora: traditional group dance, celebratory
Kasha varnishkes: buckwheat groats fried with bowtie noodles
Kibbutz, kibbutzim (pl): Community of people voluntarily living and working together non-competitively
Kina hora: superstitious saying, to warn off evil, like "knock wood"
Kishka: Eastern European sausage
Kitsch: description for something garish, tacky, low-brow
Kneidlach: another word for matzo ball, or dumpling
Knish: traditional Ashkenazi snack food, baked or fried dough filled with potato, cheese, sometimes spinach
Kugel: noodle casserole, sweet with cheese and sometimes fruit
Kvetch: complain
L'chaim: traditional toast, "to life"
Latke: potato pancake, fried, traditionally served during Hanukkah
Ma Nishtana: the first two words in a phrase recited on Passover, meaning: "Why is this night different from all other nights?"
Menorah: candleholder used at Hanukkah, typically has

8 branches for candles and a ninth for the candle that lights each

Mensch: Yiddish for a "good person," a "stand up guy"

Mezuzah: parchment scroll in a decorative case, contains a prayer and is hung in the doorway of many Jewish households, etc.

Mishegas: Yiddish for foolishness, silliness, craziness

Moshav: a type of cooperative farmers' village in Israel

Ope: midwestern slang similar to "whoops" or "oops"

Oy vey: expression of exasperation, or dismay

Pelmini: Russian dumplings

Polke: a chicken thigh, although sometimes used as a Jewish expression (comparison) over a baby's chubby legs

Rosh Hashanah: Jewish New Year

Sephardic: Jewish person of Spanish/Portuguese/N. African descent

Shabbat: The Jewish day of rest, the Sabbath (the seventh day) observed beginning sunset Friday to sunset Saturday

Shadchan: matchmaker

Shamash: candle used to light the other candles on the menorah

Shayna punim: "pretty face"

Shiva, shivah: meaning 'seven' - the law of mourning someone

Shtupping: having sex

Sufganiyot: deep fried jelly doughnut eaten during Hanukkah

Tashlich: meaning 'cast off,' an atonement ritual during Rosh Hashanah of throwing bread crumbs into flowing water to symbolically cast off the sins of the previous year.

Tevye: character (father) in the play/musical "Fiddler on the Roof"

Treife: non-kosher food like bacon, shellfish, etc

Tzedakah: a moral obligation of charitable giving, although the word actually means "justice" - doing the right thing by helping people in need.
Ulpan: classes/program to improve your Hebrew language skills
Verklempt: choked up, emotional, touched
Yarmulke: Yiddish word for skullcap/headcovering worn by Jewish men and some Jewish women. Also called a kippa/kippah in Hebrew
Z"L: people will write this after a deceased person's name, stands for *zikhrono/zikhronah livrakha*, meaning "Of blessed memory, may he/she/they rest in peace"
Zayde: Grandfather

Printed in Dunstable, United Kingdom

73895623R00109